Luca meets Bella and have a one nightstand. In the morning she disappears and he has no memory of her or the night. Four years later he runs into her…and his twins.

December 2012
Luca:
It's morning. I'm in a strange hotel room. I vaguely remember returning last night after hitting the bar downstairs, but there's something else prickling at the recesses of my mind.

***

Four Years Later

I see a figure off in the distance, it sparks something in my mind I don't know what, I don't know this person; do I?
As I draw closer my breath speeds up, my skin prickles and the hairs on my arm stand on end. I grow light headed, you turn around, your eyes grow round and then you try to hide behind your golden brown hair.

"Mommy there..."
Wait you have a kid, who are you, why do you seem so familiar...the kid, why does he look...
I stop in my tracks, I know that face I see it every morning in the mirror.
"Momma..."

I turn my head to this new interruption, there's another one, a little girl...I look at you as the pieces start to fall into place. It all comes flooding back, that night I wasn't too sure of, that night that has haunted me for nearly four years almost to the day. The dream I've been chasing. But it wasn't a dream, it was real, you are real.

"Who are you?"

A Family for Christmas
Jordan Silver

Discover other titles by Jordan Silver

Bad Santa

SEAL Team Series
Connor
Logan
Zak
Tyler
Cord
The Lyon Series
Lyon's Crew
Lyon's Angel
Lyon's Way
Lyon's Heart
Lyon's Family

Passion
Passion
Rebound

The Pregnancy Series
His One Sweet Thing
The Sweetest Revenge
Sweet Redemption

The Spitfire Series
Mouth
Lady Boss
Beautiful Assassin

The Protectors
The Guardian
The Hit Man
Anarchist
Season One
Season Two

Eden High
Season One
Season 2

What A Girl Wants
Taken
Bred

Sex And Marriage

My Best Friend's Daughter
Loving My Best Friend's Daughter

The Bad Boy Series
The Thug
Bastard
The Killer
The Villain
The Champ

The Mancini Way
Catch Me if You Can

The Bad Girls Series
The Temptress
The Seductress

Other Titles by Jordan Silver
His Wants (A Prequel)
Taking What He Wants
Stolen
The Brit
The Homecoming
The Soccer Mom's Bad Boy
The Daughter In Law
Southern Heat

His Secret Child
Betrayed
Night Visits
The Soldier's Lady
Billionaire's Fetish
Rough Riders
Stryker
Caleb's Blessing
The Claiming
Man of Steel
Fervor
My Little Book of Erotic Tales
Tryst
His Xmas Surprise
Tease
Brett's Little Headaches
Strangers in The Night
My Little Farm Girl
The Bad Boys of Capitol Hill
Bad Boy
The Billionaire and The Pop Star
Gabriel's Promise
Kicking and Screaming
His Holiday Gift

Diary of a Pissed Off Wife
The Crush
The Gambler
Sassy Curves
Dangerously In Love
The Billionaire
The Third Wife
Talon's Heart
Naughty Neighbors
Forbidden
Deception
Texas Hellion
Illicit
Queen of My Heart
The Wives
Biker's Baby Girl
Broken
Indiscretion
The Good Girl
The Forever Girl
Biker's Law

Jordan Silver Writing as Jasmine
Starr
The Purrfect Pet Series
Pet
Training His Pet
His Submissive Pet
Breeding His Pet

Jordan Siler Writing as Tiffany
Lordes
American Gangster
Double The Trouble
http://jordansilver.net

Kindle Edition, License Notes

Chapter 1

BELLA

***

I smiled as I heard the pitter patter of little feet rushing down the hallway to my room. I stole one last snuggle under the warm down comforter as I psyched myself up to roll out of bed and face the day.

I could almost feel the cold floorboards under my feet and that first brush of cool air that will inevitably come when I leave the comfort of my bed. A New England winter is not for the faint of heart, but I can't imagine living anywhere else.

Couldn't imagine giving up the tree lined streets and moose munch grass covered in snow. Frozen lakes, and ski slopes.

"Momma…mommy." My twin son and daughter came flying into the room and on to the bed for their morning hugs and kisses. I soon forgot all about the cold and misery that I would soon face as I enjoyed the innocent love of the two little beings that owned my heart.

No matter what else the day may bring, there was no better way to get it started. I inhaled their scent and stole a few more hugs before the tickle monster attacked amidst fits of glee.

I fought my way out of the tangle of arms and legs and caught my breath.

"Okay kiddos, mommy has to get ready for work." I dragged out of bed and found my ratty old house slippers and slipped my feet into them as I had a child hanging off of each leg. Their wild giggles and chortling helped to ease the strain of worry I've been burdening under for the past month or so.

"Cereal time munchkins." I helped them into their booster seats making sure to strap them in safely before hitting the button on the coffee carafe and grabbing their little bowls, Ninja Turtles for Luca and Hello Kitty for Luna.

I kept everything within arm's reach of each other because I'm not a morning person on the best of days, and winter makes it worst. I checked the thermostat and turned it up one degree all the while hoping the heat wouldn't be cut off before I could get my overdue payment in.

I poured the kids their cereal and turned the radio on to drown out the noise of my own thoughts. The sweet melody of holiday music filled the air and my babies clapped their hands in approval. One day when they're old enough to understand, like maybe when they're twenty-five, I'll tell them why they were so in love with the season, the day.

I smiled wanly at the memory that I try hard everyday to forget, which is next to impossible since all I have to do is look two feet away at one or the other of them to be reminded.

How could I ever regret something that had given me these two? Sure life could've been easier had I known…but now was not the time to dwell on such things. It's Christmas, or close to it anyway. Time to put on a happy face for the kiddies. No sense in spoiling their fun.

"Jingle bells, jingle bells…" my three-year old daughter started singing her favorite Christmas carol along with the radio as her brother grinned at her indulgently. He's such a gentle boy, so calm, at least when it comes to his sister. I sometimes wonder where he'd got that calm demeanor. It certainly wasn't from me. And I didn't know enough about his dad to know if it was he who had passed that on to his son.

I sipped my coffee as we had our usual morning conversation that included lots of repetition, but I didn't care, I loved this time with them. They were growing so fast I knew any day now it would be time to send them out the door to the school bus. I felt just a little sadness leave me at the thought. I better soak up all these moments now then I guess, because I didn't see any more babies in my future. Shake it off Bella.

I checked the clock and saw I had a little less than an hour to get out the door for work. My mom should be pulling in the driveway any minute now. "Come on kiddies mommy has to have her morning shower."

"I want TV." My little princess fought with the restraints on the seat with no luck and I knew if I didn't get over there in the next second and release her there would be hell to pay.

Unlike her brother, she was not the most patient sort and she wasn't shy about letting her displeasure be known. "Not right now Luna you know the rules." I never let them out of my sight not even for a minute. When I'm in the shower, I leave them on the bathroom floor mat playing with their toys, that way I can see and hear them through the curtain.

They were soon going to be too old for that, but for now it was the best I could do. I flicked off the water ten minutes later feeling at least half alive as I headed back to my room to get dressed. The little ones followed behind having one of their conversations that no one else could ever understand, making me smile from the heart.

This time of year was always a little harder for me. While everyone else was rushing around with their shopping and party planning, I was barely going through the motions. If not for my babies I would hide myself away from the rest of the world and rejoin the living sometime in February.

It was ironic that the best things in my life came from this season, and yet it was so bittersweet, because there was something missing, someone. I let my mind drift only for the barest of seconds. I had found with time that it wasn't wise to let my thoughts linger too long on him and what where or who. It was getting harder as time went by though. And this year seemed to be harder than the last two combined.

Each new thing the twins did would set the memories raging, but nothing got them going quite like this season. I heard mom pulling up outside and snapped out of my reverie. I hurried into my boots grabbing my purse as I rushed out of the room. I'd gotten so lost in thought I hadn't realized how much time had passed.

I knew that wasn't the end of it that the memories would plague me until this blasted season was over and done with, and there was nothing I could do about it. "Hi mom." I kissed her cheek as I made my way to the door while she greeted the kids.

"Hi sweetie, and how are my little darlings this morning? Did you miss grandma?" She knelt to hug each kid in an arm and not for the first time I gave thanks that she was here for me.

If not for her, the last four years would've been hell. She'd really stepped up, helped me to see that it wasn't the end of the world to be forced to give up your dreams. Now when I look at my kids, I wouldn't have changed it for the world. Well maybe that's not entirely true, but there was no point in wishing for things that could never be.

"Don't forget Bella, tonight is Santa at the mall night."
"I know ma, you're dropping them off around five. I gotta go, call me." I rushed to my old car and barely missed landing

on my ass when I slipped and slid on the icy ground.

I slammed the door and wished for a better car. I hated having to drive my kids around in this death trap. The heat only worked when it felt like, and the mechanic's price was too high. Either four hundred dollars or my body for the foreseeable future. No thanks. At least it was clean.

The thought of the night ahead was depressing but I knew the kids would get a kick out of it, like they have the past two years. As much as I wasn't looking forward to the hustle and bustle of battling other parents and their kids to get in line to see the jolly old fella, the glee on their faces would be worth it.

I pulled into the parking lot of the office building where I was currently employed as a paralegal with three minutes to spare. "Huh." I sighed hard as I got out and prepared to face Mr. Grabby hands. If I didn't need the job I would've kneed him in the balls a long time ago, but my babies needed to eat.

There was Christmas music coming from the storefronts of the other businesses in the complex and someone had a seven-foot tall Santa blowup that was blowing back and forth in the wind. Every window, every pole within sight was decorated in one way or another.

"Good morning Isabella, don't you look…fresh this morning." I mumbled a good morning and slipped past him hoping he didn't put his grimy hands on me. You'd think with all the news about sexual harassment in the workplace he'd know better, or at least hesitate to be such a douche.

But I guess since his daddy was a big man around town he thought he could get away with it. Plus the fact that he was a lawyer, he was sure to know his way around any kind of lawsuit. I think it was more that he knew I was desperate and not willing to make waves. Bastard!

I sat behind my desk and got right to work, not giving myself time to think about anything but getting through this day and the next. I ignored the decorations and bows of holly and ivy, was even able to block out the low hum of Christmas carols that were piping through the speakers.

I can't wait for this holiday to be over so I can go back to my crappy life without the added distraction of fixating on a man who probably forgot me the minute he woke up the morning after.

Chapter 2

LUCA

***

The ringing of the phone intruded on my dreams and tore me out of a deep sleep. "Dammit." My eyes popped open and for the first few seconds I was still caught in the dream. I'd been so close this time. I felt the loss like a live thing as I rolled over to pick up the phone.

"Aren't you on the road yet? You know we're expecting snow tonight." "Hello to you too ma." I laid back and rubbed the last dredges of sleep from my eyes. Shit, I wasn't looking forward to this conversation. For the past three years, she's been begging me to come home for the holidays. I've been able to avoid it thus far but I got the feeling this time she wouldn't be taking no for an answer.

"Look ma, I was thinking…"
"Oh no you don't son. You're not going to lie to me one more time. Four years, that's how long it's been since I saw you in person and this year that computer screen just isn't gonna do it. Besides, I've already told everyone you're coming." I could hear in her voice that she was fighting back tears and it tore at my gut.

She was right. I've been skating by with excuses for a long time now. In fact I'm surprised she'd let me get away with it this long. I hated like hell to disappoint her but she knew…

"Son I know-I know they say time will heal all wounds but that's just horse pucky. But you need us you need family, especially this time of year. We're hurting too you know. We loved them Luca. It's breaking my heart that I lost you when we lost them, please come home to your family."

She knows just how to get under my skin. It's never been easy for me to deny her anything. But was I ready to face them-To be in a room filled with my past? I never wanted to step foot in my hometown again, never want to walk in old places that held so many memories. It was easier this way. At least it used to be. For some reason this year seemed harder than all the others. Even the dreams were more vivid and with each one I came closer to remembering.

"Won't you do this for me son? Just give it a try. If you don't like it I won't ask again." I felt bile start a slow burn in my gut and gritted my teeth against the now familiar feeling. I waited for the nausea to pass before giving her an answer.

"I'll be there ma." I didn't stay on much longer after getting an update on everyone and their lives. I still had that between sleep and wake feeling and though I knew there was no way I would go back to sleep. The dream felt better than the cold hard world. Why not hold onto it a little longer?

I wasn't surprised that my morning wood was a little harder than usual. It's been that way for a week. I got that quick flash of memory again and waited to see if there would be more this time. Every year it was the same thing. As soon as the holiday cheer started floating through the air, the flashes would start. Taunting, tormenting because after almost four years I still didn't know what they meant.

I knew it wasn't the loss of my family. That was a different kind of pain. That pain was stored in a whole other compartment of my living hell. But where the pain of that loss has started to ease with time, not by much, but it's got to where I can think about the wife and son I'd lost without wanting to die myself.

This other seems only to intensify with time.

Four years of teasing glimpses of memories that I had no recollection of. Memories that seemed too real to be anything but. They left me feeling bereft, empty. As if I'd left a piece of myself somewhere, which made no sense.

Four years ago, my wife had hit a patch of ice on the way home from holiday shopping right after Thanksgiving. Our three-week old son was in the car with her, and I was at work, running late as usual. There was always a deadline to meet, always, another day another time to do the things that I should've been putting first all along.

Then it was too late and they were gone. After that the things that I had once thought I needed were the first things I left behind. It was as if I blamed my life for what had happened. I'd fooled myself into thinking that I had been doing it for them. Going the extra mile so that I could be the best, get the best jobs, a reward or two here and there in my field.

Now the ones I wanted to be proud of me were gone, and I realized too late that they would've much rather have had me there than all the other things I gave them.

I remember burying them. I know I stayed sober long enough to do that. Then there is a period of about three weeks when everything is a blur. But the worse was Christmas. I know I wanted to avoid that day and anything that had to do with the festivities. Abby had liked the holidays. That's why she'd gone out to catch a sale at the mall with her sister, even after I'd asked her not to, that I'd go the next day and pick up whatever it was she was after.

She'd assured me she was fine, and me being preoccupied with work had stupidly let it slide. Four hours later I was standing on the side of the road looking down at what was left of them in the wreckage. To this day I can't stand to see car lights reflected on snow.

The town had been decorated since the day after Thanksgiving so there was holiday shit everywhere, and the music. I can still hear the song that was playing in the car when I got the news. I pushed those memories away as I climbed out of bed. It wasn't those that bothered me now anyway, and I did feel guilt over that.

Almost from that first year, this other memory had somehow taken the place of the ones of my family. Not that I didn't mourn them, I did for a long time. But these other memories somehow kept teasing at the edges of my mind, taking my focus off of everything else.

All year, I may get a little zing here and there, but nothing like around this time. I'd be going about my day and suddenly a scent would hit me, or I'd hear a song, some little thing that would trigger a memory that went nowhere. All I know was whatever was playing at the edges of my mind had to be very important for it to have been with me this long.

The last thing I remember about my last night in the town where I'd grown up is showing up at a bar. I'd been on my way out of town, feeling sorry for myself. The bar was a mere hour or so outside of town, but that was as far as I'd gotten before the snow had started coming down too heavy to see out the window.

Lucky for me it was a hotel bar, if you can call the shabby two story building that, but it was either that or take my chances on the road under the same kind of conditions that had pretty much taken the lives of my wife and kid.

I remember taking a seat at the bar. I remember ordering a couple and then…that's where things get hazy until I woke up the next morning. I woke up reaching for my wife. In those first few seconds, reality hadn't hit home yet, and things were back to the way they used to be.

There was a warm spot next to me in the bed and my body felt like I'd gone all night. It had been a while since we'd done that. Not since…but wait, she wasn't healed yet. What had I done?

My eyes flew open and that's when reality came flooding back. Abby and Sam were gone. So why did I feel like I'd been with a woman? And what was that hint of sweet vanilla in the air? On the sheets…on me? I'd laid in bed feeling like the biggest bastard in the world when the truth finally hit.

It was obvious from the dried pussy juice on my rod that I'd been with someone. I could still smell her, feel her, but I couldn't even remember her face. Had I picked up a hooker for the night? That wasn't my style, not even before I got married, and wasn't something I ever thought I'd be interested in, but what else could it be?

If the guilt didn't kill me the hangover from hell almost did. No wonder I couldn't remember anything, the inside of my mouth tasted like horse shit and my head felt like the little drummer boy was going to town. I guess I'd had a little more than too much the night before.

I'd left the hotel and left the area as I'd planned, moving a few hundred miles away, and hadn't been back since. I couldn't stand to see anyone. There were too many memories attached to them, and the town. I knew it didn't seem fair to some, but I really didn't care back then.

I spent the first year and a half mad at the world and not caring much about anything. I buried myself even deeper in work after I realized it was the only thing keeping me sane.

I excelled in my new hometown where I was able to avoid the looks of pity and constant questions and reminiscence that I couldn't avoid back home in the small town where everyone pretty much knew everyone else.

It was easy to get lost in the hustle and bustle of New York City where everyone was too busy going about their own hectic lives to pay much attention to the plight of others. Here no one knew the story, not unless I told them and I had no plans on ever doing that.

I kept the memory of my wife and son alive in my heart, but I couldn't bear to talk about them with anyone else. My boy hadn't been alive long enough for me to have more than a handful of memories, but what I did have was enough to make his loss heartbreaking.

I've been doing more than alright for myself here in my new life. If you can call a man who hasn't done anything more than work and more work in four years living. But it's what I had and what I was comfortable with. When it was all said and done, after I'd out-ran survivor's guilt, I'd got my life back on even keel.

Except for this time of year, when everything slid out of control and my life took this surreal turn that even after all this time I had no real answers for. No matter what I did, how I tried to waylay it, come this season, those memories fought for dominance in my head.

I poured my first cup of coffee and moved my neck around to get rid of the kinks as I walked bare-assed to the bathroom down the hall.

I'd gone with an apartment instead of a home once moving to the big city. New York was certainly very different from New Hampshire. I'd never had much interest in moving here, though I'd had offers straight out of M.I.T. I was at heart a small town boy.

When I was younger and for the first two years of my marriage, this time of year was the best. There's nothing like small town New Hampshire in the winter and for the holidays everyone went all out. Streets were lined with stately homes each one more elegantly decorated than the last as if in some silent competition.

There were parties and sleigh rides, kids building snowmen on front lawns, all the things that make the holiday great. And those were the very reasons I'd stayed away so long. This time of year there's nothing but holiday cheer, and merriment all around. Neighbors have no real boundaries, and this time of year the walls really do come down.

They still hold to a lot of the old traditions, which mostly revolve around children, and I'm sorry I've just not been in the mood to see everyone else enjoying their wives and kids while I played odd man out. I didn't think it was fair of me to spoil their holidays by trying to pretend something I hadn't been ready for. But maybe ma was right, maybe four years was long enough.

Chapter 3

BELLA

***

I'd fielded the usual dozen or so phone calls from mom throughout the day, evaded my boss's roving hands and read the want Ads on my lunch break the way I have been for the last few months. I knew it was wishful thinking. The only way I would find a job that paid as well as this one was if I moved away and that just wasn't possible.

My support network was here. Well now it only included mom and dad, everyone else had their own lives after all. But those two had been more than enough. I was working and putting away every penny to try to get my kids out of the hellhole we were currently in. My parents had offered to make room for us more than once, but I needed to stand on my own two feet.

We'd stayed there right out of hospital because I needed all the help I could get. But after the first two months things between my younger sister and I had soured even more than they already were, and it became unbearable to be there any longer. Especially when she started turning her discord on my children.

Melissa had always had some kind of weird competition going on with me in her head since we were kids. She was two years younger, but way worldlier than I was. When I'd shown up pregnant after only a year and a half in school, I was terrified. My sister was very pleased. She was only too happy to rub my failure in my face every chance she got.

And I guess the fact that mom and dad had stood by me and done everything they could to make life easier for me, had not sat too well with her because she'd just become even more obsessed with the time they spent with me or any help they extended.

Everyone tiptoed around her because for a while during her fourteenth year she'd gotten mixed up with the wrong crowd and had dabbled with drugs and begun her sexual experimentation.

When it had all come out in the open my sister had become suicidal. The shame had sent her into some kind of psychotic break and it hadn't helped that the whole town started their comparison game then.

Before all that, I knew people had whispered behind their hands about the differences between the Clifton girls. But after that whole mess they were no longer whispering and their words only served to fuel whatever resentment she already bore against me.

So she was rather pleased when Saint Bella as she was fond of calling me, messed up and got herself with child. For a man that she couldn't even name no less.

I'd been honest with my parents about that even though I knew they might share it with her, we were family after all. I was hoping she could put our differences aside and just be there for me during what had to be the scariest time of my life. But no such luck.

Of course I'd always been there for her, no question, but she didn't see the need to be there for the sister who she believed had always overshadowed her since she was born. She was beyond angry when our parents stepped in and helped in every way they could even with their limited resources. She thought I should've been kicked out of the house and all their love and attention given to her.

But my parents had done all they could for me, and the twins. It wasn't that we were dirt poor, but we weren't rich and certainly hadn't made plans for two new babies on the horizon so soon.

I'd used most of the college fund dad had put aside to help with things for the twins and used the rest to take the paralegal course.

Melissa been even angrier once I continued my studies, going for the paralegal certificate instead of the law degree I'd been after before I was waylaid by the unexpected pregnancy. I guess in her mind I was finished now that I had kids.

She'd made life at mom and dad's unbearable for me, and the kids, so I'd had no choice but to move out on my own. Though mom and dad had argued against it, I could see that it was lifting a strain off their shoulders.

Melissa was their baby after all, and all she need do is bring up the fact that they did more for me than they did her to get them backpedaling fast, even though there was no truth to her assumptions.

It's been four years and she too now has a little boy who's barely a year younger than my twins. And still she can't give up this sick competition. Still trying to make my life difficult.

I shook those thoughts off as I made my way outside. Mom should be pulling up any minute with the kids. I guess my mind was moving in those circles because of the holidays.

Outside the air was clean and brisk, with a few flurries already swirling in the air. You could actually feel the Christmas spirit. There were bells going off in the distance, the church bells that the town will be ringing every hour on the hour until after the New Year.

There was red and green on every pole stretching as far as the eye could see going down Main Street. Not to mention the silver and gold streamer and tinsel decorations that hung across the street with messages of Christmas cheer.

As I sat there watching people going about their evening, as the sun was about to make its descent in the sky, I felt that strangeness again. Every year about this time, it happens. I get the strongest urge to go back there, to see if maybe…

Maybe what? Maybe he'd come looking for you? Maybe you two could have some kind of fairytale happily ever after? I'd stopped reading romance novels because I no longer believed in such things. But every year for the last three I've secretly held out hope for my own little miracle.

I wonder if he ever thought of that night. How was it possible for two lives to be so drastically changed and one not even know it? I'd never resented him for leaving me with my little Christmas surprise, after all had I not been attracted to him I never would've gone up to his hotel room, never would've let him undress me…

I always grew very uncomfortable at this point in my trip down memory lane. For whatever reason, this time I forced myself to remember. It wasn't like the memories were fading anyway; they only seem to get stronger with time. I sat in the car staring straight ahead as my mind went back in time almost four years to the day.

I'd been pushing it to get home in time for Christmas morning. I'd stayed late at school to finish up a term paper. By the time I got on the road for the three-hour drive home it was already dark out and there were flurries of snow in the air. Had I taken the time to listen to the weather report, I would've known there was a freak storm headed in the path I was about to embark on.

Mom had been too busy getting ready for the festivities to be her usual stay on top of every minute detail self. Usually on my weekend trips back home I would've gotten a complete rundown of every road construction, downed tree and any other impediment one could run into on the road.

I'd made it to just outside of town, maybe twenty-thirty minutes, when my car had almost skid off the road on a patch of ice. It was the weirdest thing because I didn't think it had iced or snowed that hard yet. But just like that the floodgates opened up and the flurries that had been following me for the past couple hours became a blinding blanket of white.

The only sensible thing to do was find the nearest place for warmth and shelter and lucky for me there was an old hotel right up ahead. I'd never stayed there before, never had reason to since it was just outside of town. It was a quaint little place, one of those boutique New England hotels with loads of charm and history. I guess some might find it outdated, but for an old romantic like myself, it was the perfect setting for a romantic holiday.

The lobby was practically empty with everyone tucked away safely in the warmth of their rooms, probably with their noses pressed to the windows enjoying the real experience of a New Hampshire Christmas.

It really was rather picturesque once you got over the bitter cold against your cheeks. Snow covered pine trees with just the softest glow from the old fashioned street lamps was like a throwback to a Dickens tale come to life.

Chapter 4

BELLA

***

I took a seat at the bar, staying close to the very end. I wasn't old enough to drink and didn't want to bring attention to myself, but the elderly bartender had been all that was kind and taken pity on me. He'd even got me a cup of hot chocolate and sent me to the little sitting area where there was a fireplace and a table with cookies and other little holiday treats for their guests.

That's where I'd seen him for the first time. Just sitting in a darkened corner of the room, so still I wouldn't have known he was even there had I not been admiring the Christmas decorations and following them around the room with my eyes.

"Oh, sorry, I didn't realize anyone was here." I took a seat since my legs were about to give out. It wasn't because like in one of my many romance novels his eyes had mesmerized me, or any such thing. I couldn't really see his eyes.

It was more the sudden fright that had made me lose my breath. That and the way he just seemed to watch me. I'd been in there a good three minutes before noticing his presence, had he been watching me that whole time?

Though I couldn't see his eyes to gauge color or expression, I could see the glare of the fire reflected in them and with his rugged build and his face in shadow, it seemed rather ominous. When he raised his hand I almost fell off my chair until I realized he was lifting a glass to his lips.

That's when I noticed the tray on the table next to him with the bottle of something amber inside.
"I'm sorry, I didn't mean to intrude…" I stood to leave, sure that he was obviously a guest looking for solitude while I was a mere intruder who had no right.

"Sit." The one word wasn't slurred, neither was his voice heavy with drink. But that's not the reason I dropped back into the chair. It was because I felt as though I couldn't disobey. My heart picked up speed and I curled my fingers into my palm to control the sudden trembling in my hands.

There was something in his voice; in the way he seemed to just watch me from the dark. I didn't get the serial killer vibe from him, but I sensed danger all the same. My heart I remember, had beat unusually fast and my pulse had gone into overdrive. I imagined that he could hear the harsh breath as it sawed in and out of my lungs, like I'd ran a marathon.

We'd sat there, both of us silent, me gazing into the fire even though I could feel his eyes on my face, staring. My face heated up from more than the fire in the grate and I dug my nails into my palms to keep myself steady and calm. Then his voice had come out of the dark and I'd almost jumped out of my skin.

"Why are you out in this?" Somehow, although the question was directed at me, I kinda got the sense he wasn't really talking to me. Then he'd continued his conversation. "Don't you know better than to be out on a night like this?

"I…" I started to answer when I caught the edge of anger in his voice. Maybe this hadn't been such a good idea after all. "No, don't go." How did he know that I was about to get up and go take my chances out in the car?

The bartender had told me he would be leaving soon for home and the lobby was closed until morning. I would be here alone with this stranger. The warm Christmas cheer from the piped music and the fire dancing in the grate was suddenly tinged with fear.

Then he'd started to talk, more calmly of everything and nothing. His voice lost its edge and suddenly I was at ease. He'd asked questions but somehow it seemed that he wasn't really hearing the answers. Still I sat there and listened. There was something in his voice. Some hint of sadness, and I guess the whole experience was too ethereal for my overly imaginative mind to ignore.

"Come here." I still don't know why I'd gone. Why I'd left the comfort of the overstuffed smoking chair and gone into that dark corner to take his outstretched hand. It wasn't like me. Not level headed strong opinionated me. But that night as if in a trance I'd gone to him and in the faded light from the window where he sat I'd seen him for the first time.

He was gorgeous. Even though his eyes were a bit bruised and sad, and there was a touch of sullenness to his mouth, he was by far the most gorgeous man I'd ever seen in my life.

I knew he was a man and not a boy by his build and the way he melted me with a look. I'd put him at about thirty to my nineteen and a half. When he took my hand and turned it over in his, butterflies took flight in my stomach. Such an innocent touch, but it packed quite a punch.

"What is your name?" He had a New Hampshire accent with a tinge of something more cultured, something that made things happen in my body that seemed to be centered between my thighs.

"Isabella, but everyone calls me Bella." He ran his thumb over my palm and then looked at it as if wondering how it had gotten there. I was about to pull away gently and go back to my seat when I found myself on his lap.

My heart beat wildly with a sudden pang of fear. What had I gotten myself into? The bartender was long gone and I was all alone in this darkened room with…

"Don't want to be alone tonight, please don't leave me…" his hand was on my nape while the other rested on my thighs. I don't know why I didn't pull away or scream or hit him, anything to get out of his grip. But when he'd pulled my head down to his I was helpless to stop him.

It was my first real kiss and it was a doozy. In the end I was the one clinging, the one taking his tongue deeper into my mouth, the one who didn't even want to come up for air. I didn't object to his hand cupping my breast through the thick sweater, in fact I wanted to drag it out of the way and feel his hands on my naked flesh.

There was a strong taste of alcohol on his tongue that wasn't unpleasant in the least but only added to the headiness of the kiss and I got sucked under deeper and deeper. My skin burned with need and that hand on my breast became a sweet torture. I wanted badly to feel the warmth of his flesh against mine.

He seemed to understand, seemed to know as he stood to his feet dropping the now empty bottle to the carpeted floor and lifted me into his arms effortlessly. I didn't see where we were going, wouldn't have cared. In that moment, I wasn't in control of myself. It was as if something or someone else had taken control of my senses and all my usual cautions went out the window.

I didn't feel fear, there was danger yes, but of a different kind. I knew I was about to do something that would change my life forever. It was monumental and this certainly wasn't the way I'd seen myself losing my virginity. But somehow,

I couldn't seem to stop what was about to happen, or want to.

He closed the door behind us with his foot and took me to the bed across the room. Even the room was a like a stage set for seduction. There was a fire blazing in the stone fireplace that took up half of one wall, and a large bear skin rug laid on the floor before the fire.

The room was toasty warm and the smell of pine from the garland hanging from the mantle along with the lights peeping through the windows from outside made it feel as if in that room we were wrapped in a cocoon of warm holiday cheer. Certainly nothing could go wrong.

His hand went beneath my sweater and broke my train of thought. It felt so strange there, where no one else had ever dared. His big, callused hand was cool against my warm skin and the contrast sent shockwaves throughout my body. But nothing, like when he lifted my sweater and tore my bra out of the way to put his mouth on my already turgid nipple.

"Ohhhh." The sound was wrenched from me. I could no more have held it back than I could've stopped him. He made love to my nipple. I looked on in amazement at he way he licked, then nibbled then suckled. And when his hand came up to hold my breast in place for his mouth, I felt a gush of liquid heat between my thighs.

I wanted, no needed to feel him there. It was all so strange, so unreal. As if I were watching things play out from afar. Seeing myself do these things that were so out of character and yet powerless to stop myself.

Once again, as if having access to my mind… my thoughts-just when I thought I would go mad from the emptiness between my thighs, he rolled his body over, pressing me down into the mattress. Blocking me from escape, but most of all, pressing that rigid hardness between his thighs into me just where I needed it most.

I exploded, lifting my body hard into his, wanting more of the feel of him. My hands held his head in place as he fed at my breasts, now exchanging one for the other as he ground himself into me and I came and came until my breath was gone and I laid limp beneath him.

He pulled his mouth away from my nipple and his hands were at my waist, on the band of my slacks. This is it; this is the point of no return. This is when I should stop him and get back to my car where I could sleep off this strange feeling that had entrapped me since walking into this place.

But instead, I lifted off the bed so he could drag my pants and underwear down off my legs and over my shoes. When his mouth came down between my legs, the scream got trapped in my lungs. Never, never did I ever imagine that anything could feel this good.

He didn't just put his mouth on me the way I always imagined it was done. He delved into me with his tongue. His hands took hold of my hips and he held me in place for the onslaught of his mouth, driving his tongue into my depths over and over while he made the sexiest noises I'd ever heard anywhere.

Then he'd stopped with his tongue buried inside me, and his fingers manipulating my clit, as bursts of light went off behind my eyes. He growled something and I felt the reverberation enter me, setting off little explosions deep in my womb.

I was too caught up to think straight. My body, me senses had taken over. The whole night had become something from one of my romance novels. It didn't seem real. It was as if I was caught in a surreal dreamlike adventure from which I would awaken in the morning and all will be back to normal again. But no dream had ever felt this real, this amazing.

He climbed up my body after nipping my inner thigh and we shared my taste in a kiss that was so intoxicatingly sweet it brought tears to my eyes. Who was this man that knew my body better than I? Who touched me with such reverence that I felt it in my very soul?

I felt his hand between us, as he struggled with his belt, and the feel of his fingers brushing against me left me hungry for more. I lent him a helping hand as our mouths clung together passionately. I tasted myself on his tongue and the taste inflamed me more. By the time he was free of the confines of his pants I was ready to beg him to put me out of my misery.

When he slammed into me, my body went into shock. The sharp pain brought me back from the peak of the mountain where I'd only just been soaring. But it was the look on his face, of surprise and disbelief. "How?" He shook his head as if to clear it before easing himself slowly, gently out of my body as if he would leave me, but he didn't.

Instead, he stopped with just his tip inside me as he took my nipple between his teeth again. Liquid heat rushed from my body and made it easy for him to slide back inside.

By then the searing pain between my thighs had dissipated, and that powerful feeling of lust was rebuilding stronger than before.

Chapter 5

BELLA

***

It was I who pulled his head down to mine, me who moved my hips under his, me who led one of his hands back to my neglected nipple. He took things over from there, moving into me like he couldn't help himself.

"So tight, so sweet. Never let go..." He mumbled a whole lot of sweet nothings that kept my pulse racing and my body heated and so wet it was almost embarrassing. He was a magnificent lover. I knew that even though he was my first experience. I'd read enough about the subject to know, and beyond that, the way he made me feel was nothing less than mind blowing.

He didn't just use my body for his own pleasure, wasn't selfish. He took me to great heights not only with the way he used his massive cock to wring the most magnificent pleasure from me, but the way he touched me so tenderly, and his kiss.

I knew his appendage was larger than average because of the way part of him still hung outside of me and I was already full. I could feel him deep inside me, the pleasure pain caused by more than just my maidenhead that he'd just ripped to shreds.

His teeth in my neck brought my mind back into sharp focus and set off new tremors that ran through me. The way he lifted my ass in his hands as he brought me into his thrusts had me wrapping my legs around him and digging my nails into him as my mouth hung open in shocked surprise and pleasure.

He sped up his thrusts and his grunts got louder as he pounded himself into me over and over until the pleasure was too much and all went dark.

I awakened to him sitting next to me with a wet cloth pressed between my thighs, easing the sting from what he'd done to me. He saw my eyes open and threw the cloth to the floor before climbing back over me again.

Only this time, he turned me around and put me on my hands and knees, before sliding back into me with my hair grabbed tightly in his fist.

If I thought this had felt good before, nothing compared to having him take me like this. He was even deeper in me now, and the things he did with his free hand. He ran it from my nipples to down between my thighs where he was stroking in and out of me. His teeth marked my neck and shoulders as the tugged on my hair hard enough to sting, but the pain only added to the intense pleasure.

"I love fucking you like this, love the way your ass feels cushioned against me. Open your legs let me feel your clit." I spread as he pulled me up so that my back was against his chest. "Put your arms back and around my neck. That's it." He dropped my hair and now used both hands on my body, one on my nipple, one between my legs.

I was stuffed from behind as he moved my body with his and growled instructions in my ear. "I want you to squeeze down around my cock. That's a good girl. Now flex your pussy muscles, I want you to drag my seed from me; come on." I had no idea what he meant but I did as he asked and the pleasure was indescribable.

It seemed to be good for him too, because the next thing I knew he pushed my head down into the mattress; kneed my legs apart, and drove himself into me so hard my neck almost snapped.

He pulled my head back by my hair but kept my upper body pressed into the bed with his as he fucked me. There was no other word for it. The other may have had a tinge of lovemaking to it, but this, this was pure animalistic coupling.

Even his grunts and growls had changed. They were now wilder, harsher, his words more explicit as he told me how much he enjoyed my body and what he was doing to me, in me.

Now I was a little afraid, not so much of him as of the feelings he'd unleashed inside of me. They were out of control, all consuming and for an innocent like me, almost terrifying. I felt like I was falling from a very great height and all my senses were centered in that one place between my thighs.

He took me over completely his hand coming up to wrap around my throat as he slammed into me. Oh dear heaven he'd cum inside me last time and there was nothing between his seed and my womb.

I should stop him as I felt his cock expand inside me as if getting ready to cum again, but I didn't want the sweet feelings deep inside me to end.

He did something new, twisted his hips at an angle and sparks flew. I forgot all about protection and danger as I lost all sense of everything else other than the feel of his thick length inside me. Battering away at some place deep inside that made my body respond even wilder than before.

"Don't stop, don't ever stop, please…" The words were torn from me, as I got lost in a fog of lust and love so profound it defied logic. How had I ended up here in this time and place? How was this total and complete stranger making me feel these things?

Not even the steamiest of my romance collection could have prepared me for this.

And he wasn't through. Whoever he was, he was very good at this. The way he played my body. I felt the loss when he pulled out but I wasn't left feeling empty for long because soon I felt the coolness of his tongue as it searched my depths once more.

My eyes rolled back from the pleasure and I gripped the sheets in my tight fists as he made love to me with his tongue and fingers before driving himself back into me. "Tell me you want my seed." The words almost made me swoon as my womb contracted and I told him what he wanted to hear.

"Yes, please." He grabbed hold of my hips and his pounding jerked my body to and fro as he chased his climax and my body and mind exploded in a maelstrom of violent ecstasy that once again left me at the brink of the dark abyss.

I held on this time, this time I felt his release as it jetted into me. Felt the sting of his teeth as he bit into my flesh with his orgasm that seemed to go on forever. He held me then, bringing his body down to cover mine as our hearts fought to get back to their usual pace. His arms around me felt safe, like I belonged there…

***

The beeping of a car horn brought me back to the present. My hands clung tightly to the steering wheel in a death grip until my fingers were almost numb. My heart raced in my chest and it took me longer than usual to get myself back under control. There was a dull pain throbbing between my thighs that was more than a little frustrating since there was no way in hell for me to ease the ache. I hadn't been with anyone since that night, hadn't even had the slightest urge.

No, these days all my lovemaking was done in my dreams, in the reliving of that one spectacular night of the most amazing lovemaking that I was sure no reality could ever hold a candle to.

I shook off the last vestige of my lust filled haze as I got out to help mom transfer the kids from her car to mine. One of the things that had made my sister crazy was the way my parents had gone all out for the twins when they were born, and then again when I'd moved out of the family home.

Mom had insisted that they get car seats of their own because she knew what a drag it would be to have to constantly move them back and forth from one vehicle to the next. Days like today I really appreciated it because though there was still some light left, the day had grown colder.

"Hi kids, are you all excited about seeing Santa?" They were they usual exuberant selves at seeing me after hours of being separated, and the added bonus of getting to see the jolly old guy had them all but jumping in their seats as mom helped me strap them in.

"Why were you sitting out here in this cold car? Why didn't you wait inside?" I never told her nor will I ever about my boss the octopus. It would only make her worry and I'd given her enough of that for a lifetime.

"Oh, you know me, you know how much I love this time of year. I just wanted to sit and look down Main Street at all the decorations, see everyone going about their holiday madness."

She bought that yarn and dropped it for which I was immensely grateful. I have been very good at keeping my lackluster feelings about the season hidden thus far, and having to make the day special for the kids had helped. But the truth is, I wish I could just magically ghost through the days until it was all over.

"Okay, don't forget to take lots of pictures and we'll see you at the house tomorrow for wrapping." She called as she got into her car. Oh gripes, I'd forgotten all about that little tradition. Every Christmas eve, the kids and I spent the night with mom and dad where the adults stayed up well into the night wrapping gifts for under the tree in between cooking and baking for the next day.

"Okay mom, thanks again." We waved our goodbyes while my two little angels prattled on in the back, filling me in on their day. For them I swallowed my ennui and put myself into the spirit of things. We sang carols on the way as we enjoyed the spectacular scenery of lawn displays and window dressing. The big day was only two days away and the whole town was going full steam ahead.

Chapter 6

LUCA

***

"Ma I agreed to be here, I don't recall agreeing to going out and about in town." That was the last thing I needed. I'd convinced myself four years ago when I left that it was best. I could avoid all the well wishes and condolences, but I'd only been back a few hours and already I could see the error of my ways.

It was as though everyone had stored up their words of sorrow and the intervening years didn't seem to make a difference. I'd already had enough so if she thought I was stepping foot off this estate until it was time to leave she was nuts.

"I need that fudge for the party tomorrow night. Your sister was supposed to pick it up but she got stuck at the office and your dad has his hands full at the hospital. It's just a quick run to the mall in Manchester."

"That's what I don't understand, why couldn't you get fudge here? Why do I have to go more than an hour away in this mess?" I was dragging on my boots even as I griped halfheartedly at her.

"I will have you know that that horrible Millie Thorne served their fudge at one of our teas just last month and it was all the rage. Now she thinks she has one upped me since she refused to say where she got it."

"So how do you know she got it there?"
"Easy. I got Aggie to ask her cook and voila." Aggie was her personal servant and her damn spy. It used to be a running joke in the family that the kids had two mothers. What ma's friends didn't snitch, the servants of the other families would tell Aggie and there would be hell to pay.

"So now, I'm off to where is it again?"

"The Mall of New Hampshire. It's in Manchester. Don't speed son and take your time. Walk around I hear they do a spectacular job at the holidays. Take some pictures. I bet it's a sight to behold. And son try to enjoy." I rolled my eyes behind her head but didn't argue. I kissed her hair before heading out to my truck.

I'd flown in on my private jet and had a truck waiting for me at the airstrip. I didn't let myself think of the drive ahead. I'd avoided the town of Manchester for a reason. It was there that I had awakened that morning four years ago in the rustic little inn with no recollection of the night beyond checking in.

I started up the truck and resigned myself to the trip ahead. If the memories hadn't become clear after all this time there was no reason to believe they will now. I guess I'd just have to put them away now and move on.

It wasn't until that very moment as I drove towards the town that I realized that night was the reason I hadn't been able to truly move on. Yes, the grief and sorrow of my loss had held me back some. But in four years, I haven't been able to even look at a woman and there had been plenty offers.

Each time I felt the need, or even came close to inviting a woman into my bed, that night would raise its ugly head and I'd be left alone with my thoughts and a nagging feeling in my gut. If I knew who she was, I would've searched her out, but I had no idea where to start. All I had was the memory of her scent, but not even so much as the color of her hair had stayed with me.

For all that, she had a hold on me- my mystery woman. For a while there, I questioned if every woman I met could be her. I didn't know who she was but what about her? Did she remember me, or was I just one in a long line of lovers? For all I know, she had gone on with her life while I have been stuck in limbo.

Maybe when I return to New York, I'll try to put this behind me and live a little outside the office and my workroom. Maybe it was time to shut down these memories and release myself from the strange hold they have over me.

I'd only mentioned the memories of that night to one person. They'd suggested hypnosis of all things but somehow it felt wrong to remember that way. If that night did happen, then I wanted those memories to come to me.

I'd already put aside the guilt of sleeping with someone else so soon after losing my wife. I had no doubt that it was the alcohol mixed with grief that had led me down that road. So though I'd borne some guilt in the beginning, I'd long forgiven myself.

I guess the hardest part for me was not knowing. I'd got myself tested after that night and came up clean, but there was no doubt in my mind that I had made love to this woman whoever she was, without protection. It was evident by her juices that had dried all over my cock.

I made it to the mall in record time and sat in the over crowded parking lot gearing myself up to face the madness inside. It had been a while since I'd been to a mall or anywhere shopping for that matter. These days, I had a personal assistant who took care of those things.

In the four years since my life had been torn apart, I had put even more of myself into my work. After the move to New York, I had thrown it all in and it had paid off. Between investments and trading, I'd landed a huge contract my first year there. The developer who'd had an interest in my work since college was only too pleased to learn I was headed his way and decided to snap me up before anyone else got wind of it.

What had started out as one job had turned into a full fledge partnership that spanned a few continents around the globe. I purposely kept myself busy so that I never had time to think. Now, at thirty-four when other men were settling down to family life, I'd already done my stint and was never going back there again. That was something I had on the new up and coming architects in my field I guess. I had no distractions, no obligations other than the job.

Since I now headed my own firm with my name on the door, it didn't really matter because I called the shots. Now when my family was gone, I had all the time in the world and nothing to do with it. No one to spend it with.

I slammed out of the Mercedes G-Class when my thoughts were getting to be too much. I'd rather face whatever madness was going on in there than sit out here with my own thoughts.

Two things blasted me in the face as soon as I stepped out onto the snow-covered ground. The loud Christmas carol that escaped each time someone opened the door leading into the mall, and the cold wind that carried flurries of icy snow with it.

Pulling up the collar of my cashmere jacket, I headed for the door, my only thought of getting in and out. I braced myself for the hit to the gut and kept my eyes focused straight ahead. I'd Google checked the store location and knew exactly where I was going and had no plans on stopping in between.

There were a million kids dragging their mothers or fathers by the arm, all seemingly headed in the same direction and I did my best to stay out of the way. Jingle bells rock blasted from the speakers, lights winked on and off from every available surface and there were about ten decorated Christmas trees in the one hallway I was now walking down.

I saw the great attraction when I turned the corner and saw the huge sleigh up ahead surrounded by fake snow and reindeer. The man who sat there, reins in hand, looked like everyone's imagination of what his namesake should and I guess it was a toss up between whether it was him or the mountain of gift wrapped goodies in sacks at the foot of that sleigh that was the cause of all the hullabaloo.

I had to go by all that to get to the candy shop, but at least they were trying to have some semblance of order with the line- forming thing. I was halfway past the line that stretched the length of one hall and wrapped around to the other when I got that prickling feeling.

I almost stopped in my tracks. But I knew it was only because I was here...in this town- at this time. It's the reason I was set on avoiding this place. Somehow, I knew the feelings would be stronger here, especially now so soon to the anniversary of when it happened.

I ignored the sensation of being close to something monumental and hurried my pace in the hopes of getting to the store and picking up ma's orders quickly and getting the hell out of here. The farther down that hallway I went the more I felt it. I looked sharply around for anyone that may be looking my way but that wasn't so easy in a crowd this size.

Something caught my eye as I perused my surroundings. There was a figure up ahead in the distance. I couldn't see much but the golden locks of her head. That hair, with the lights from the trees glancing off of it sparked something in my mind. I don't know what, I don't know this person; do I? Still my feet kept going as if without my permission.

As I drew nearer, my breath sped up, my skin prickled and the hairs on my arm stood on end. I grew light headed, as if I were about to pass out. Some part of that night flashed behind my eyes and I knew I had to stop this person whoever she was. I knew it was a woman from the hair, but the ugly wool coat that swallowed her small frame hid her body.

There was something about her height, the way she moved her body. As I got within a few feet that sweet vanilla scent hit me, and the world spun. My rod grew hard instantly and I reached out to touch her shoulder. She turned around, and her eyes grew round with the surprised look people get when they see something they're not expecting.

She looked down and away suddenly, and tried hiding behind her golden brown hair.
That action seemed so familiar, but why? Her face, though beautiful, wasn't known to me. Yet I could swear I had seen her before. I think I already knew who she was, but it was so far fetched as to be unbelievable. What were the odds that I would run into my mystery woman my first night back?

She bit into her lip and it was as if the floodgates just opened up. I stumbled back a step as I kept my eyes on her face.

Afraid to look away lest she disappear again. I tried to say something but my tongue wouldn't work and my heart was beating me to death.

I looked at her as the pieces started to fall into place. It all came flooding back, that night I wasn't too sure of. That night that has haunted me for nearly four years almost to the day. The dream I've been chasing.

But it wasn't a dream, it was real, she was real. I stepped into her space getting as close to her as possible, my hand came up and around her neck, holding her in place so she couldn't run away. Her scent hit me hard this close and my body reacted like a well-trained dog, pissing me off.

"Who are you?"

She opened her mouth to speak but no words came. I kept my eyes on hers as more became clear. Flashes of memory hit me behind the eyes like a movie reel. We were in bed…but how did we get there? Did I pick her up somewhere? She didn't look like a working girl. Then shit got really strange and my world was rocked for the second time in my life.

"Mommy there…" I looked down at the little boy who'd just spoken but everything seemed like a jumble. I knew there was something monumental going on here in this moment, but I couldn't get a handle on it. I stared down at the kid fighting to make sense of what it was my brain was trying to tell me.

Wait, she has a kid, that doesn't fit somehow. But how do I know that? Who are you, why do you seem so familiar...the kid, why does he look...? I looked down at the little dark haired boy again and this time the cloudy haze had cleared. My mind stopped in its tracks, and the word stood still. I know that face I see it every morning in the mirror.

I looked at her in shocked horror as the buzzing in my ears drummed out the Christmas carols and the chatter in the background. I was about to speak once I found my voice but once again I was interrupted.
"Momma..."

I turned my head to look down at her other side at this new interruption. There's another one, a little girl...with my face. I felt the earth shift beneath me, and my head begun to spin. In between the black dots that appeared behind my lids, I saw flashes of her and I in bed, naked. I was inside her, deep inside her. Even now my body reacted so strongly. And there's that scent, vanilla and something tropical. "You…"

Chapter 7

BELLA

***

The world stopped. I knew there was life going on around me, knew there were people moving in and out of my peripheral vision. But for me everything had stopped and rewound itself back to that hotel room. He was asking me something but I couldn't hear his words, just saw the movement of his lips and the anger on his face.

It was only when my outgoing little girl pulled on his pants leg and he got down on his knees to talk to her that I snapped out of it. I was ready to make a run for it. It was obvious from his questions that he didn't remember me or who I was, probably not where we'd met and what we'd done either. I kinda expected that because of something else that had happened that night. Something I never let myself think about because the shame and humiliation was too much to bear.

It was only when he'd rolled away from me that last time as the sun climbed above the snow capped mountains that I realized he'd been too intoxicated to know much of what had happened throughout the night.

"They're mine aren't they?" He stared at me with a mixture of anger and hope, and as much as I'd wished for this moment in the past, I now wished it never happened. "This isn't the right..." Before I could finish speaking he picked Luna up in his arms and took Luca's hand with the other.

"What are you doing? Where are you going with my kids?" There was no doubt about the look he turned on me this time. Pure anger, hate and a whole host of things I wasn't sure I wanted to decipher.

"Lady, you have a lot of explaining to do. And since you were the one calling the shots for the past four years, I'm not about to risk you disappearing again." He walked as he spoke, and I moved to take my son's hand to keep some semblance of control over the situation.

I followed him to the candy store where he gave the lady behind the counter a name. Deleon. Was that his last name? Last time I'd only got his first name and only because in one very amorous moment he'd said 'Say fuck me Luca.' Which I had repeated more than once, I might add, and most of the time without any prompting from him.

My heart raced with this new little tidbit I had to add to the keepsake I kept in my head with all that I knew about him, which wasn't much. Somehow, I found humor in that. Here I was the mother of his children and I had no idea who he was.

He paid for the boxes of fudge and with my son's hand still in his and my daughter in the other, turned and looked around. "Is there a place where we can sit and talk?"

"There's the food court but I doubt there'll be any available chairs. It is the holidays after all." I can't believe my voice is so steady, like I was having a normal conversation with an old friend I just happened to run into.

"We'll see." His voice was clipped and short and it would take a stump not to see that he was beyond pissed. "Let me take her you have your hands full." The bag with boxes of candy was hanging off his hand under Luna. "Not on your life, walk."

I had no choice but to follow him, all the while wondering when my life had turned into a soap opera. What were the odds that we would meet here again like this? I stayed out of Manchester, only venturing into the city when there was absolutely no other alternative.

As I suspected, the food court was packed but there was one little table in the corner. He headed there and I followed close on his heels.

I tried taking Luca back from him but he beat me to it and put the child on his lap with Luna on his other knee. "So what's your name little buddy?" The soft congeniality of his voice belied the daggers he was sending my way with his eyes.

"Luca." I saw his reaction in the way his shoulders stiffened and then he picked his head up and his eyes bore into mine. Luca, who was normally a little more reticent than his sister when it came to strangers, seemed perfectly relaxed and at ease. I on the other hand was a bundle of nerves.

"I have to get back, it's getting late." He reached across the table and grabbed my hand.

"First, you're going to tell me what I want to know. Are they mine?" I couldn't bring myself to say it. I'd imagined this moment a thousand times, but now that it was here I couldn't seem to get it together.

"I asked you a question." He seemed so different to the man who'd made love to me all night. Though he'd been forceful in his lovemaking, something that had given me many moments of remembered pleasure, his words had been more of a gentler persuasion.

"What makes you think…?" I was stalling for time. If I took this step there was no turning back. I never realized until now how much I hated the idea of sharing my children. There were times alone at night in bed when I'd dream of him coming and taking us away. I knew he was wealthy from the clothes he wore that night and the expensive watch on the night stand the morning after.

Though money wouldn't solve all my problems, it didn't hurt to daydream about my knight in shining armor coming to the rescue. Now he was here and I didn't know what I wanted.

"Don't play games with me. They both have my face."

"Do you really not remember?" I had accepted the possibility but after all this time shouldn't some of what happened that night have come back to him?

"Lady, until roughly ten minutes ago I thought that night was a figment of my imagination. For four years I've been haunted by little flashes of something, always out of reach and not enough substance to know whether it was dream or reality."

I guess I could believe that, not like I had a choice. But what did this all mean? He was here now, but what? In my daydreams we walked off into the sunset and lived happily ever after. But the man sitting across from me with a look of leashed anger didn't look like he was going to conform to my way of things.

"Why did you leave?"

"What?" His question threw me for a second.

"I woke the next day and you were gone, that's why I never knew for sure if you were real."

"You called me by someone else's name. I couldn't bear to face you after that." There was no point in not coming clean now. Though this whole thing seemed surreal, I knew there was no way he was going to let me leave here without…something.

"What name?"
"Abigail." His sharp intake of breath had me biting into my lip. Maybe I shouldn't have been so honest. Oh shit, what if he was married, what if our one night together had been a betrayal? And why hadn't I ever thought of that in all this time?

For some reason it never entered my mind. Somehow, I had developed this ideal of him, and part of that ideal was that he wasn't the type to cheat. I had no answers for why he'd called me by someone else's name, but I knew it was me he was touching that night, my body he used so beautifully.

***

LUCA

***

It was true then. How else would she know my wife's name? "Tell me about that night." She looked down at the kids meaningfully and I got the point. The kids-my kids were busy talking to each other and not really paying us much mind. But their little ears were still too close. I didn't really need her to tell me what I could see with my own two eyes- what I already knew in my heart. But I wanted to hear the words all the same.

"Right, we need to go somewhere quiet and talk. Where do you live?" Her look of surprised panic was almost comical. I could've told her that it didn't matter to me one way or the other because the second I realized these kids were mine, I'd already started rearranging her life. Shit, did she have some other man raising my kids? I'll kill 'er.

"Are you married?" The words pissed me off even farther but I'll have to examine why later.
"No, not many takers for single women with twins these days." I could've told her that most men would overlook all that for a chance to be with someone who looked like her, but now was not the time.

Just beneath the surface of the more obvious issue on the table, was the constant throbbing pain of an erection. The last time I'd had one of those induced by something more than the dream, was the night we'd spent together. The night that was becoming clearer the longer we sat there and with that clarity came a sense of peace. I'd found her.

"Is there some place you need to be? Someone waiting for you?"
"No, just my mom and that's tomorrow."
"Good let's go." I got to my feet and picked up both my son and daughter giving her no choice but to follow.

The mall was in full swing now as people took advantage of the late hours for the holiday season.

There was laughter and holiday cheer all around us. So amazing that no one here knew how life changing this moment was for us. That others were going about their lives while we were on the precipice of something that will change ours forever.

Chapter 8

LUCA

***

Once outside and the cold air hit me, and the magic of lights and decorations faded, all that was left was the reality. Was this really happening? And how was I so calm about it? I think I was still processing. There was too much still to put together for me to go off on one of my rages. Plus my kids were seeing me for the first time even though they didn't know who I was, and I wouldn't do anything to scare them, not for the world.

I followed her to her car with the intention of following her home, but one look at the vehicle and something inside me seized in revulsion. "You're not driving my kids anywhere in that." It was a piece of crap. There was rust on the doors and the tires didn't even look remotely new. All I saw as I stood there looking down at that travesty was my wife and son wrapped around a tree.

"I'm sorry? This is the only car I have. It's been getting us around pretty good until now." My anger came back full force. While I was dining on the best steaks and finest wine, driving the best cars on the market and enjoying the best life had to offer, my kids were driving around in this piece of shit facing certain death.

I don't know all the particulars of what had happened, why she'd ran and not tried to find me once she found out that she was having my kids, but there was no excuse.

I turned and headed in the opposite direction looking for my truck. "Where are you going? You can't just take my kids." She followed behind me pulling at my arm and almost fell. "Be careful you little fool." I waited until she righted herself and kept going.

We had one problem when we reached my truck. "We'll have to go back and get the seats from that death trap. You sit in back and hold them." I kissed both my kids' hair and put them in the backseat before climbing into the driver's side.

I drove slowly across the snow-covered lot, taking constant peeks in the rearview mirror at the two little heads in the backseat. There was so much going on inside me at once it was hard to hold onto any one thought.

I wanted to call ma and tell her the news, wanted to take them home with me and never let them out of my sight again. And what's stopping me? Their mother maybe. My eyes went to her. There was still a lot missing from that night, but it was all coming back now in bits and pieces.

We reached her junk heap and I got out to get the seats. She didn't have much to say after I shut down her first try to stop me. She'd learn soon enough that once I was set on a course nothing could stop me. Once I had transferred the seats and got the kids settled with me again, I just sat there.

"Where do you live?" She took her time answering but she finally did and I put the address in my GPS before heading out of the lot. I'll have to call ma soon so that she didn't worry, but right now my only focus was on getting to the bottom of this.

There was only one thing I was sure of. I had two babies. What had their lives been like without me there to protect them? And the woman who now occupied the seat next to me? What kind of mother was she to my kids?

They looked healthy enough but what did I know? My son hadn't even made it to a month before he was taken from me, and before him I hadn't had much to do with kids. Luca and Luna, she'd named my kids after me.

"If you knew who I was why didn't you tell me about them?"
"I didn't know who you were."
"Don't lie to me. How the fu...how did you name them after me if you didn't know?"

She went quiet and I think she was blushing but wasn't sure. "You told me to call you Luca." No, that wasn't exactly right. I saw it as plain as if it were now happening. I was inside her, I told her to beg me to fuck her. Why did I call her by my wife's name? How had we ended up in bed together? That part was still a little hazy. The only thing I could remember is being inside her. Everything else was still blurry, the memories spread all over the place.

I needed to concentrate on the road so I'd have to hold the questions for later, but before the night was over I will know everything. The GPS alerted me that we had reached our destination and I almost turned the car around and left.

"Here, you raise my children here."
I looked over at her and saw the look of
shame on her face. Maybe I was being too
hard, but I was beyond pissed that this
was my kids' life. I could offer them so
much more. Why had she done this to
them, to me? What was her fucking game
anyway?

I got out and opened the door to get
my son. She followed suit and grabbed
our daughter. Our daughter, I had
children with this woman, this total
stranger. What kind of woman had sex
with a stranger in a hotel room? That was
unfair I know, but I was too pissed to
give a damn about what was fair and
what wasn't.

I still had too many unanswered questions, and I hated being at her mercy for all the answers, since it seemed my mind could only recall our lovemaking. I followed her around the side of the little bungalow looking building with the chipped paint and hanging shutters.

I looked at my watch and it was already late. "Pack some things for you and the kids, they're not staying here." I guess that was the wrong thing to say because it seemed to get her back up.

"Listen, I appreciate that this has come as a shock to you. Trust me, it's no picnic for me either, but you can't just expect to come into our lives and turn everything upside down. It's late, the kids are tired and they need to go to bed."

"And they will, just not here." She wasn't too pleased but that was to be expected. This was hard for both of us, but I couldn't think about her feelings or mine. All that mattered was the safety and comfort of my kids.

There was no textbook manual for this situation, no guidelines for me to follow. I'm sure the reality hadn't quite set in yet, but I knew one thing for certain. I'm not letting them out of my sight… none of them.

I don't know why or how this happened. Well that's not entirely true, the little flashes of memory were telling me how, but for whatever reason this…miracle was taking place, it was mine and I'm not about to let go.

"I'm sorry but you have no say in this." And shit like this was not helping the situation. She obviously honestly didn't know anything about me.

"You wanna bet?" I walked through the little rundown dump in search of the children's room. I knew there could only be one because the place was too small to have more than two bedrooms.

I must be coming across as a real asshole to her, but she had them for three years. Three years when I didn't even know they were out there, needing me. The thought hurt my heart and sadness overpowered the anger. Three years without me in their lives and the looks of this place and that thing she calls a car told me all I needed to know about what those three years were like. Was I to blame for this?

I can't think about that now though, I can only make things right. And I knew just where to start.

It never entered my mind that they weren't mine. All I had to do was look at them to see the evidence. Not even my siblings resembled me that closely. I knew what I was doing as I put one foot in front of the other going down that hallway. I wasn't allowing myself to think. The last time I didn't pay attention I ended up standing over my family's grave. Fuck if I'll let that shit happen again.

She followed behind me with the little ones toddling along. I did notice one thing; they were very well behaved kids. They'd been quiet all the way here except for some kind of language they shared between each other. But there hadn't been any screaming matches no whining. Nothing that you'd expect from two kids who'd just been hijacked by a complete stranger. Or were they used to mommy bringing home strange men?

I looked at her over my shoulder and was surprised that the thought made me feel murderous. "Do you do this a lot?" The words barely made it past gritted teeth.

"Do what?" She looked genuinely surprised by my question.

"Bring men home around my kids." Her face heated up but along with the embarrassment there was a hint of anger. "No, I haven't been with anyone since…" She cut herself off and now it was I looking at her quizzically. What had she been about to say?

Luna pulled on my leg to get my attention and broke the spell. "Yes princess?"
"Wanna see my toys?" She did some cute little girl thing twirling around as she asked with my smile on her face. Geez, how could the emotion be there already?

Would it be clichéd to say I was already in love with them? That the moment I saw my son's little face, my daughter's, it's as if I knew. Even before she admitted that they were mine, something inside of me knew. Outwardly three years stood between us, but inside I was already their dad. I took my little girl's hand. "Sure princess.

I came to the first room and guessed it was theirs from the cartoon characters on the door. Pushing the door open only solidified my plans to take them out of there. The room was tidy enough but the window had a crack and the room was cold, the whole place was cold.

I looked back at her, not accusingly, but I was sure she saw the anger and disdain. "Get their stuff and yours you're coming home with me. Don't argue, not in front of the children." I picked them both up and left the room giving her space to do what she had to.

Ma will be going out of her mind right about now so I sat on the ratty old couch and called her while I bounced my kids on my knees. "Luca where are you? I've been worried sick."

"Ma, I'm okay, something happened." I didn't know how to tell her, what words to say. "I'm coming home and I'm bringing someone with me, someone I need you to meet." That wasn't accurate either but it was the best I could do.

I grew impatient after I hung up the phone and she was still not back, but just as I was about to say fuck it and head out the door with my kids she came into the room with a little cloth bag. It didn't take a genius to see how they were living, and that pissed me off no end. I held my tongue for now though and headed back to my truck.

"I need to get my car."
"Not tonight, I'll have someone go after it in the morning."
"What if someone takes it?" I looked at her incredulously as I got the kids settled in their seats.
"You can't be serious." That bolt of nuts was good only for scrap.

I didn't say anything more since she seemed to take offence. But there was no way my kids were ever getting in that thing again. I was aware that I hadn't let myself think of her, but was focused solely on the kids. That night we'd been together, hadn't been long after I'd buried my wife. Somehow now that she was here in the flesh it felt like a betrayal.

I had questions of course, but I had to wait until we were alone. The kids might be little but I wasn't about to have this conversation in front of them. I did notice though that my body was still responding to her nearness. It felt the way it does when I wake up from one of those dreams, only now I had a face to go with it, and the memory of what we did that night. Shit!

Chapter 9

BELLA

***

What am I doing? I didn't even put up much of a fight. He hadn't yelled or done anything threatening to get his way, but somehow I sensed something in him. It was there just beneath the surface. That same forceful manner, like the one he'd used when he'd got me to stay with him that night.

It wasn't overt, there was no menace in him, but somehow you knew not to say no, not to cross him. I wasn't used to dealing with anyone like that. He was nothing like my boss the crab. He was just a sleaze. Luca on the other hand was, masterful. That's the only way I can describe him.

I sat in the car holding onto the seat with white knuckles as he drove carefully through town and took the turnoff to the highway. "Where do you live?"

"New Castle. My family lives there, I'm just home for the holidays." Figures, New Castle is the ritziest town in New Hampshire, he looked like he belonged there.

I suddenly felt out of place and gauche. Looking down at mom's coat that I'd been wearing for the last two winters, I wished for something more stylish. At least the kids were clean even if their clothes were bargain basement.

I felt tears prick my eyes and wiped them away before he could notice my weakness. Why did I suddenly feel like a failure? Was he looking at the way we lived and making assumptions?

Outside the car window the lights and Christmas gaiety had faded. "Momma juice please?" I looked back at the kids who had been so good this whole time. What were they thinking? Why had they seemingly accepted this stranger so easily? I reached in the bag at my feet and grabbed two juice boxes. It was going on eight o'clock, way past their bedtime and I could see that they were about to droop, but the day's excitement was keeping them going.

"Here you go baby." I leaned over the seat and gave them each a juice. "Why did you stop?" I sat back in my seat to see that he had pulled over to the side of the road. "Nothing; put your seat belt back on." I did as he asked wondering about the tightness in his voice and the way he seemed to be gritting his teeth? Did he not want me to give the kids their juice in his fancy car?

"They're very tidy they won't spill."

"I don't care if they tear this shit apart with their bare hands." He looked back at the kids before pulling back out onto the street. He turned on the radio and a Christmas carol blasted into the car. He reached as if to change the station but Luna heard her favorite song and started to sing, stopping him in his tracks.

He got the strangest look on his face and I could swear his face turned sheet white before he composed himself. I didn't miss the slight tremble in his hand when he replaced it on the steering wheel and put it down to the events of the evening finally hitting home.

He must be feeling just as out of it as I am. I felt as if I hadn't been able to think clearly since seeing him again for the first time. Everything seemed to be moving so fast, like a movie on fast forward.

"Does she always sing that song?" Strange question.

"Yes, it's her favorite, sometimes she makes me play it in April." The strain eased from his face and his body relaxed. "It used to be mine too. A long time ago."

We drove for another hour no one saying anything since the kids had fallen asleep half an hour ago. It was very uncomfortable and I could imagine he was feeling the same. Where was this all going to end? I was afraid to think about it.

When he pulled into the gates of an estate I knew I was sorely out of my depths. If the kids weren't fast asleep in the back I would've opened the door and ran all the way back home but it was too late for that now.

The driveway seemed to go on forever until we came upon a house that looked like a picture out of house beautiful. The place was lit up for the holidays. I could see the ten-foot tall tree through the window and with the snow backdrop the whole place looked like a winter wonderland.

Out front the yard was decorated with reindeer and snowmen, the hedges beneath the windows covered in twinkling lights. I focused on the mundane so I didn't freak out by the sheer enormity of the place. It was massive.

"You…you live here?" my voice sounded like Luna's. Before he could answer the massive front door opened and a man and woman came out on the landing. There was no need to guess who they were, since the man had Luca's face.

They were both beaming at the sight of us and the man put his arm around his wife's shoulders. I sat like a lump while he got out and went to the back door. The movement awakened Luna who started to fuss when she awakened in strange surroundings.

"It's okay sweetheart, daddy's got you." My heart melted in my chest. It was the first time he'd called himself that. And when I looked back and saw him kiss Luna's little head I felt stupid tears forming again.

I only moved and got out of the car when he headed towards the steps with my daughter bundled up in his arms. I couldn't hear what was being said, but I heard his mother's scream when he pulled the hood back from Luna's face.

There was a flurry of movement then the barrel chested man who I'd already surmised was his father came towards the car and pulled me into a bear hug before heading for the back and Luca. I was trapped like a deer in headlights.

It all seemed so surreal. I put one heavy foot in front of the other as I followed behind him to where Luca and his mother were going into the house because she was saying it was too cold out for the children.

Unlike me, she had given free rein to her tears and was babbling on in between plastering the kids' faces with kisses. She finally noticed me and looked from me to her son. "How, when?"

"We'll save that for later ma, for now we need to get the kids settled."
"Of course son, just tell me one thing, did you know?"
"No ma, I just found them." Now he sounded like he was about to cry, and the look his mother threw me did not bode well for holiday cheer.

I followed behind the three of them like a fifth wheel, his father carrying my son and he our daughter. The front hall was bigger than the little house I was renting. I started to shake as I thought of all that could go wrong.

Now when it was too late everything that could go wrong played through my head. This family obviously had money, what if they tried to take my babies? What of they cut me out of my children's lives? What if they blamed me for not telling their son about his children?

A million horrible scenarios went through my mind as we went up the winding staircase and down another long hallway to a door at the end. "I'm sorry dear what was your name?"

"Bella." I answered his father.

"Well Bella, this is where my daughter's children stay when they spend the night." The room was a kid's paradise. It was two rooms separated by a doorway. In one room were nothing but toys with some kind of scene painted on the wall, while the other room had bunk beds and a little princess bed with canopy and enough stuff toys to fill a toyshop.

His mother still hadn't said anything to me as she fussed over the kids. "Open that drawer over there Matthew and get me some pajamas." She ordered her husband as she undressed first Luna and then Luca. I stood in the doorway feeling like I didn't belong.

It was obvious no one was saying anything because of the kids. "Pretty." Luna the talkative one raised a hand to…I guess her grandmother's cheek and patted. "Momma." She called for my attention.

"Yes I'm here sweetheart." Luca Jr.'s grandfather was busy trying to get him into the pajamas but my big boy wasn't having it. "I can do it." They all laughed and encouraged him while he showed off his big boy skills.

Luna jumped off her grandmother's lap and made a beeline for the wall of toys. "No Luna…" I reached out to stop her but his mother's soft whisper behind me stopped me.

"Luna, you named her after her father."

"Yes ma and my son's name is Luca."

"But I don't understand…"

"Not now ma, we'll tell you everything as soon as we get the kids settled."

It was another half an hour before the kids wound down but I wasn't ready to leave them alone up there so he took his parents back downstairs while I sat up there to make sure the kids didn't wake up scared.

After an hour had gone by, I couldn't put it off any longer, so I left the safety of the room to go face whatever was awaiting me.

I found them in the den where the fire was going in another massive stone fireplace with garlands and holly and ivy strung along the length of it. There was another Christmas tree in the corner of this room with red and gold balls and tinsel, and the whole thing looked like a postcard.

They all looked up when I stopped in the doorway unsure of myself. "Come in Isabella." It was the first time he'd called me by name and it felt strange hearing it come from his lips.

I walked into the room and took the chair closest to the fire since I felt cold even though the room was warm. He gave me a strange look and I wondered what he was thinking. I kind of got it when his eyes widened and he got up from his chair.

"Ma, dad we'll be right back." He crossed the room and took my hand pulling me up from the chair and leading me from the room. I was almost tempted to beg them not to let him take me. What was he thinking? Did he think I betrayed him?

"I Remember." I swallowed hard at his words and looked down at the floor. "We were in that little sitting room off the lobby in that shitty hotel. Why didn't you stop me? I know I was drunk but what was your excuse?"

"I…" What was I supposed to say? That I fell under his spell? That everything seemed lined up in the stars for what happened that night to transpire. "I've asked myself that same question a thousand times."

"You were a virgin, there was blood…I remember breaking through that thin membrane and taking your innocence."

Good grief he really did remember everything. There was nothing to say to that so I kept my lips sealed, as he seemed to work it all out in his head. He moved around the room, which looked like a study and I just stood there waiting for whatever came next.

I'd lost control of the whole situation long ago and now I was here at his mercy and for the first time since finding out I was pregnant, I felt totally lost. I couldn't get a handle on him, on what he was thinking or planning in his head. For him that night was new, I've lived with it for four years. What must that be like for him?

"I'm trying to piece this all together but you have to admit it's like something out of a movie. You didn't know who I was that night?" He said that as if it was hard to believe. "No I didn't." Saying it out loud even in this day and age sounded so crass. Good girls don't sleep with strangers. Sleep! What a crock. If only that's all we'd done that night. Then we wouldn't be here now, dealing with this.

"What were you doing there that night?" Now he sounded almost accusing as if I'd set him up. "The roads were icy, I skidded on a patch of ice and…" His whole body shook and he turned away from me as if in pain.

"Go on." I cleared my throat and told him the rest of the story. "And when you found out you were pregnant?"

"I had no way of finding you, all I had was your first name."

"Yes, I remember how you got that." The look he gave me then was nothing less than searing.

"Yeah, well, as I was saying, I didn't know anything more about you, and there was nowhere to look even if I'd wanted to."

"If you'd wanted to? Does that mean that you wouldn't have looked for me, had you known?"

"I'm not sure how to answer that. I mean we had a one night stand, a one night stand you ended by calling me by someone else's name. How was I to know you'd want to be found?"

"Sorry about that. I'm sure you know by now that I wasn't exactly myself that night." He moved to look out the window at the falling snow. "This is all so strange. I don't know if I should thank you for having them, or hate you for keeping them away from me all this time." He turned to look back at me.

"Look I didn't know I was pregnant until I was three months along. I was too sick and scared to worry about finding you when I didn't have the first clue where to start…"

"You could've found a way. You had my first name all you had to do was go back to that place and give them that…"

"And tell them what? Oh I know, hello, my name is Isabella Clifton, I've never stayed in your establishment but I stopped in one snowy night the night before Christmas and ended up in this man's room. I don't know his last name, but the first was Luca. Is there anyway you can tell me how to reach him?" I was breathing harsh by the end of that last sentence, and my famous anger had finally come out of hiding.

"Lower your damn voice." Oh wow, he did controlled anger thing very well. I had the good sense not to test him and kept my mouth shut. "You could've found a way. Do you know how this makes me feel?"

"How what makes you feel? You had a one-night stand with a woman you didn't know, were you expecting two kids in the bargain? And what about your wife? Would she have appreciated me showing up on your doorstep kids in hand? It took you less than a second to figure out they were yours how long do you think it would've taken her?"

"My wife is dead." The words were a tortured whisper that stopped me short. "Oh, I'm sorry, I didn't know."

"How could you have? That's what I was doing there that night. I was getting out of town. I'd just buried my wife and three week old son."

I dropped into the nearest chair as his words hit me. So that's why he was blind drunk that night, why he'd called me by her name. I was just a fill in, a way to ease his pain. Somehow knowing that didn't make me feel any better. It was better when I could dream that I'd meant something to him. That like me, he just couldn't help himself that night.

"What a mess." Okay that's where I draw the line. "My kids are not a mess. Why don't I just go get them and you can take us back where you found us and the mess will be gone?"

"Are you fucking nuts? I'm not talking about my kids. I'm talking about the situation. My kids aren't going anywhere. And they're sure as hell not going back to that dump you call a home."

I was on my feet ready to do battle. "My kids aren't staying here, and that dump is all I can afford for the time being. I'm working hard to get us a nicer place."

"Well, you don't have to worry about that any longer because I'll be taking care of them from now on."
"You're not taking my babies away from me."
"That's up to you, but in a few days I'm on a plane back to New York and my children will be coming with me."

"New… are you insane?" I felt raw panic in my gut because I knew he meant every word. "Where are you going?" He stopped me, as I was halfway out the door.

"I'm getting my kids and getting out of here."
"Try it." I ran for the stairs and heard his heavy tread behind me. His parents came running out of the den but I didn't stop to look, just kept going.

How was I gonna get out of here? My car was in an empty parking lot an hour and a half away. Mom, I'll call mom. Before I could do that he caught up with me at the door to the nursery and pulled me back.

"Leave them." I was already winded but he was barely breathing hard. "Let me go, we're not staying here, this whole thing was a mistake. I should never have let you bring us here."

"As if you had a fucking choice." My eyes widened at the way he grabbed my shoulders so forcefully.
"Alright, you two settle down. Son, unhand her, let's all go back downstairs and try to sort this out." His dad tried getting between us but Luca wasn't letting go.
"There's nothing to sort out dad, my children are not leaving here."

"I lied, they're not…"

"Don't." He pointed a menacing finger in my face and I buttoned my lips. "Now this is what we're going to do." He was speaking to his parents but he never took his eyes off mine.

"Dad, is uncle Thomas still in town?"

"Why yes, but I don't see…"

"Call him up, there's going to be a wedding."

"Luca I don't think…"

"I know what I'm doing ma. Dad, make the call." He'd definitely lost his mind.

Chapter 10

LUCA

***

I've lost my damn mind but I was going on plain adrenaline here and nothing else made sense. I hadn't planned on getting married ever again to anyone, not after last time. I never wanted to feel that pain again. But if she thinks I'll her leave here with my kids she was out of her fucking mind. Maybe she was crazy, how the hell would I know? But crazy or not this is one fight she was destined to lose.

I was raised around wealth and power my whole life. And though my parents did everything in their power to make sure my siblings and I never became assholes, there was no changing blood. My family has been in good standing in the country since my great-great-great whoever came over on the Mayflower.

I come from a long line of very powerful men and women who have an inbred sense of what's right and wrong, coupled with an alpha complex to rival Hercules.

Had this girl, this Isabella known anything about me she would've chosen someone else to spend that night with. She'd let me take her virginity. Every time I think of that one thing it stumps me. Why would she give me her most precious possession? A man she didn't know? It was the one thing I couldn't get over. The one thing keeping me from believing she'd played me no matter what she said.

When I'd awakened in that room and saw the blood on the sheet I thought I'd hurt myself, then when I figured out that I had been with a woman, I figured she'd got her period in the middle of whatever the hell we'd done the night before.

Following hot on the heels of that was the unbearable guilt. I'd just buried my wife, the love of my life, and already I'd climbed into bed with someone else. The fact that I couldn't remember a damn thing about that night only compounded the issue.

For a man like me, always in control, it wasn't easy, none of it. I'd closed that side of my life off, had buried myself in work and making even more money than was already in my considerable trust fund. It was always a source of pride with me that I stood on my own two feet. Even though it was hard for my parents to take a step back and let me do things my way, they'd let me and been all the prouder for it.

Now this stranger, this woman who'd borne not one but two of my children expected me to walk away from the most important things in my life.

It didn't matter that I'd only just met them, didn't matter how they came to be, they were mine. I would never leave my children out there in the world without my love and protection.

I was sure that when it all kicked in I'll have a lot to think about, but right now at this moment, there was only one thing on my mind, my children. The thought of getting married again, especially to a complete stranger, wasn't exactly high on my bucket list of shit to do. But she's the mother of my children and there was no way I was leaving here without my little boy and girl.

The only way I saw clear to do that without a legal battle, which I was sure to win, was to keep all three of them. I'll figure out what to do with her later.

Dad had left the room to do as I'd asked and while I was lost in my head ma had been talking to her, Bella. I looked at her now, really looked. She was beautiful in that classic Hollywood nineteen-fifties era kind of way. That wholesome look without the harsh androgynous thing most women seemed to favor these days.

She was rounded in all the right places. And that face, even bare of excess makeup she had a natural beauty that drew the eye. Is that why I'd taken her to my bed that night? Did I, even in a drunken stupor take notice of her exquisiteness, the fact that she didn't look like everyone else?

Even after bearing my children, she still had the kind of body most men would kill for. Funny thing is before this I probably wouldn't have given her a second glance. Too programmed to follow societal norms. But the flashes of memory told me that she was the whole package, the real deal.

I could remember the fucking feel of her ass in my hands. The way she'd moved over and under me. Fuck! I didn't want this. She was the reason I'd been celibate all these years, not my wife, not the woman I'd sworn to love. It was her fucking memory that had haunted me for four years. Her existence that had kept me from forming any type of attachment with anyone because if I even thought of making love to someone else, the memory of that night was always there, blocking, standing in the way.

And now that I've come face to face with the reality, the only question left was what now? How was this all going to play out in the end?

"So you see why this is such a shock for him, for all of us." I checked back into the here and now to hear ma explaining my behavior.

"She gets it ma, no need to explain. The whole situation is a shock to everyone, but the only thing that matters are those two little people in that room. There's no doubt that I am their father and as such I can do no less than what I am about to. You let's go." I heard the doorbell and figured it was uncle Thomas.

She didn't move fast enough so I grabbed her hand and pulled her along behind me, ignoring her orders to be let go. Ma was still putting in her plug for waiting, but I turned a deaf ear. She's been after me for three years to move on with my life, this is moving on.

Bella, Isabella tugged against her hand and I stopped long enough to glare down at her. "You have two choices in this scenario, you marry me and stay with our kids, or I take you to court and take them. Choose." It was harsh because I could see that she was a good mom, and this was as much my fault as hers, but she had to face reality. Looks like we both got the shock of our lives tonight.

She opened her mouth to argue but I cut her off. "Before you say anything, no judge will choose you over me as the best choice to raise our kids. It may not be fair, and I might be the biggest asshole in the world to you right now, but there's nothing I won't do to get back the three years I lost."

"I did not purposely keep them from you. Why are you doing this?" The better question was why wasn't she jumping at the chance to improve her situation? It was obvious I had money, and was in a much better place than her financially, so…"

"You said you weren't married."
Why should the idea of her being with
someone else make me angry? I get it; it
was the idea of some other man being in
my children's lives when I'd been denied
that honor, that's all it was.

"I'm not married."
"So what's your problem?"
"Are you serious? We don't know each
other."
"We knew each other well enough to fuck
all night, to produce two kids that needs
us both. I'm willing to do my part how
about you?"

"That's not fair. Of course I want
what's best for our children, but what if
you and I hate each other? Just because
we were compatible in that way doesn't
mean…"

"Trust me, some marriages don't even have that." I took her hand again, dragging her along behind me.

Uncle Thomas was already in the living room, snifter in hand. He eyed Isabella up and down before smirking at me. "Your father was just giving me the particulars son. Young lady, do you wish to marry my nephew?" I squeezed her hand to get her to behave.

"What if I say no." She glared at me and I had to give her points for guts. "Well now, if you say no that would take up considerable time as I'd have to convince you of the error of your ways and that might take a while. On the other hand you say yes, I do the deed and I can get back to my warm den in front of the TV where my marathon reruns of Murder She Wrote is even now playing." She'll learn to ignore his quirks soon enough. At least he got it out of his system.

***

BELLA

***

I can't believe this is happening. When I woke up this morning, sure I griped a little to myself about the cold drafty house and a myriad of other things I've been stressing over for the past four years. But had I wished this on myself? How can this be happening? Maybe I should ask the kids what they asked the fat guy in the red suit for when they wake up in the morning. Stranger things have happened.

"Don't we need some kind of license for this?" I thought for sure I had him there, but I forgot I was dealing with a man who seemed to play by his own rules. I thought it was only on TV, and in the movies, that money jumped hurdles and moved boundaries, I guess I was wrong.

"Already taken care of little lady. And it cost me a nice bottle of my finest scotch. I'll be expecting you to remedy that nephew at your earliest convenience."

"Seeing as how I got you the last case I think that can be arranged."

"Oh wait, she needs something blue and borrowed and old and…" His mom ran out of the room mumbling about doing things right and I was finally convinced that I hadn't woken up this morning and I was still in the dream.

The dream became reality when his uncle said I now pronounce you man and wife and my knees almost gave out. His family actually congratulated us, like this was completely normal. I didn't know what to do with myself after the nuptials and the toast, which his dad insisted on.

I sipped my fancy water, which was all I could keep down at this point and wondered what was happening with my life. "I have to go check on the kids." I couldn't get out of there fast enough. I needed to think, and I couldn't do it down there. I should've known he wouldn't let me go alone. He was right on my heels.

"I'm not going to nab them and run. I don't have a car remember?"
"I want to look in on them too. Do they usually sleep through the night? I don't want them to wake up and not know where they are." It was on the tip of my tongue to say something catty, like he shoulda thought of that before bringing us here and holding us hostage, but I didn't.

We snuck into the room quietly and walked over to Luna. She was fast asleep with her thumb in her mouth. "I used to sleep like that." He ran his finger over her hair and I don't know why the simple gesture should touch me so deeply, but it did.

I watched him out of the corner of my eye as he looked down at our daughter. There was a mix of love and uncertainty on his face and I wondered what was on his mind. Putting aside my own feelings, I had to admit this couldn't be easy for him either. I can't begin to imagine what he must be thinking or feeling.

He looked just as I remembered from that night, even better. There were no shadows in his eyes, no haunted look. He was the picture of the quintessential eye candy. His dark hair was still worn short and those eyes, eyes that had peered at me through the dark, were the bluest blue. Just like our son's and daughter's.

They'd got all of him and very little of me in the bargain. I guess if I'd searched him out at some point in life it would've been easy enough to prove that they were his. Did he always have those shoulders, those arms? Somehow he looked more toned under the obviously expensive sweater than he had that night.

Not that he had been anything less than a ten, but he was knocking hard at ten plus. My face heated when he caught me staring. "You don't have to look away Isabella, it's all yours now."

"What? This is a marriage in name only." Kind of like closing the barn after the horse was already out, but whatever. "Think again sweetheart. I haven't fucked anyone in four years because I couldn't get you out of my head. Name only my ass. You spoilt me for all others. Just as an aside I should warn you, I have four years to make up for. Think happy thoughts when we go to bed tonight. Then again, from what I remember, you won't need to."

And with that the crazy man I'd just hitched my wagon to walked over to the bottom bunk across the room and pulled the blanket higher over our son.

I stood there wondering why his words didn't freak me out. If I was being honest I already knew. Almost from the first second I saw him in that mall my body was in heat. The whole evening was a script for a cheesy B-movie. I could've fought harder, could've not taken him home with me, and the kids. But some part of me knew that I wanted…something.

"While you're doing all that thinking over there, remember, my life has been changed too not just yours. Since we've found ourselves in this situation, I suggest we both make the best of it. It might take some time. We have to get to know each other, but if you accept what is, that would make it a hell of a lot easier. I have."

"That's the problem, how can you? We just met a few hours ago. Already you've taken my kids and forced me to marry you. Doesn't that strike you as a bit rash and unnatural?"

"No, it doesn't. Nothing about the way we met, or what happened since then is what I would call the norm. But ask yourself this. What's the alternative? You're the mother of my children. By your own words there aren't that many takers for women with kids. I don't see you living the rest of your life as a nun, and I'd be fucked if some other man is going to play any part in my kids' lives."

"What if I was already married, or dating someone?"

"But you're not so the question is moot."

He had an answer for everything, and most of it made sense for now, but what about tomorrow after he's had time to think?

"You said you never had any plans to marry. Why couldn't we have, I don't know, shared custody or something?"
"What, with me in New York and my kids here? Not a chance."

"What is it that's really bothering you Isabella."
"I don't know. I guess it's the way you're taking this so calmly. The way you seem to have all the answers."
"Would you prefer that I rant and rage at you? Not my style. I'm a doer, something else you'll learn about me. I don't argue I just do what needs to be done. Let's go, we don't want to wake the kids they need their rest. They had a long day too and tomorrow they get to learn that they have a father."

"Did you ever tell them about me?" Yeah I can just imagine that conversation. "No, not really."

"What did you tell them when they asked about their daddy?"

"I lied, I always told them that one day daddy would come home." Shit, I guess I did wish this on myself. But I only told them that to avoid the hard questions.

I started to head back downstairs not really looking forward to rejoining the family gathering when my hand was caught and I was turned in the opposite direction. "This way." My heart knocked against my ribs when I realized where he was taking me. I tried in vain to pull back but his hold was more forceful than I thought.

Once behind the door, which he closed and locked, he pulled me around to stand in front of him. "Now, I think…" He pulled my sweater off over my head. "We need to reacquaint ourselves. I figure it's best to get this out of the way so you don't spend the rest of the holiday worrying about it." He dropped my sweater to the floor and walked me backwards towards the massive bed.

Say something Bella; stop this. My rational mind pleaded but my traitorous body was already igniting. Still, I had to say something. I couldn't just give in to this. "What are you do…?" His mouth came down to cover mine, swallowing up my words of rejection.

Just that quickly I was back there in that hotel room. Nothing had changed. We were picking up where we'd left off. The same riotous sensations wreaked havoc with my senses.

Then his hands came around my naked waist and I forgot to think. The feel of his tongue in my mouth was so familiar. He wasn't playing fair either, it's as if he knew that giving me even a second to think would bring this to an end, so he didn't give me time to think.

Instead, he pressed my body into the bed beneath his while discarding the rest of my clothes. He reared up once long enough to pull his own sweater off over his head and it was I who reached for him, running my hands up his chest until they clasped behind his head bringing his mouth back to mine.

Where was this hunger coming from? Sure I've had urges over the years. Urges that I always ignored because I wanted more than just to scratch an itch. What was it that he'd said? I'd spoilt him for all others? What would he say if he knew the same was true for me too? That even the thought if being with anyone else had left me cold? Somehow I knew that no one else would compare. Or maybe I'd just built that night up in my head to such proportions that it was hard for any real flesh and blood man to live up to it.

His tongue in my mouth cut my thoughts off and I gave in to the feelings. Not like I had a choice. It seems this one man had the power to make me act in ways I wouldn't normally. All he had to do was put his hands on me and I become a wanton.

I felt his hardness between my thighs and my body answered with wild need. The world tilted as he shifted us around, bringing me to sit on top of him. "I remember these." His hands cupped my breasts as he gazed at them with a smile.

"I can see where my children changed you, you're fuller here. Feed them to me." He looked into my eyes as if daring me and I leaned over ever so slowly until my nipple grazed across his lips. Just his tongue came out for the barest touch, and my skin prickled with heat.

"Did you nurse my kids?" Why was he talking? He'd removed his pants and I could feel the warm heat of his thighs beneath me and something hard, wet, soft, hot, all those things, pressed into my back. "Yes."

His fingers came down on my clit right where I needed to be touched and I felt like I would explode. "Please."

"Please what? Tell me." I shook my head and pushed my nipple back into his mouth. I couldn't say the words, but maybe I could tell him with my body.

"You have to be very quiet while I fuck you. We don't want to wake the babies now do we?" What was he talking about? The kids were down the hall. Had I been that noisy that night? My face was on fire with the memory of just how boisterous I had been. Somehow I had blocked that out of my mind.

Even now the soft growling purrs that emanated from my lungs were starting to grow in volume. I couldn't help it, he was even better than I remembered and that was saying a lot. He ran his hands down my middle until both thumbs converged between my thighs where he tormented my already swollen clit.

My newly reawakened body was like a puppet on a string, following wherever he led. His fingers dipped between us and pierced me so sweetly my eyes closed from the immense pleasure. With the thumb of one hand on my clit and the fingers of the other stroking into me, he fed on my nipple like he was starved for it.

I moved against his hands as I bit into my lip to keep the wild sounds from escaping. But there was no help for it when an orgasm suddenly hit. He dropped my nipple and dragged my mouth down to his as he lifted me and sat me on his cock.

We both held still as if remembering, as if reclaiming something that had been lost. "That scent, I remember it, you're so wet." He turned us over then so that he was over me looking down, and then he moved. Merciful heavens. "Ohhhhh." He filled me completely.

Last time, I remember not being able to take his whole length, this time my body relaxed enough to take more, but still it wasn't all of him. But what there was of him inside was more than enough.

I was no longer thinking about that night. There were no more excuses, this is what I wanted what I wanted the minute I saw him again tonight.

"Do you remember this? Huh?" He took my mouth before I could answer and drew me down deep into the abyss. I felt those same stirrings. The same overwhelming need for this man and only this man.

As he moved in and over me, I couldn't imagine how I'd lived without this so long. "You're cumming already, I like that." He took my nipple into his mouth and my body flew among the stars. His hand came down over my mouth and the echo of my scream shot around the room.

I didn't care, didn't worry about who could hear. In that moment nothing else mattered but that these feelings never stop. "Don't stop Luca please don't stop."

"I won't baby, I promise." The way he wrapped his hand in my hair as he pulled my head back, the way he looked down at me as he stroked into me, was the sexiest thing I'd ever seen.

My eyes clouded over with lust and my vision blurred on his gorgeous face while deep inside I was on fire. I didn't care when his teeth bit into my neck even though I knew it would leave a mark. Didn't care about the sweet sting between my thighs as he pounded into me harder and harder.

"Fuck; you're so tight." He gritted his teeth and pulled out but I knew what came next and was moving into position before he asked. "That's my girl. You remembered that this was my favorite way to take you."

He ran his hands between my thighs, cupping me and I felt his teeth nip my ass cheek. By the time he knelt behind me and slid in deep I was already out of my mind. "Fuck me fuck me fuck me…"

My mouth hung open wide as he did. My body felt like it was being split in two, the pleasure pain keeping me on the edge of constant orgasm. "That's a girl, keep cumming on my cock. Like that." His hand came down on my ass hard and I screeched as my body gave him what he wanted.

"I'm cumming-I'm cumming-I'm cumming…" It was a litany of unbridled lust and when his hand came around and cupped my breast I pushed back hard taking just a little bit more of his hard cock inside me.

His body shook and I felt him grow between my walls just before I felt the sweetness of his ejaculate inside me. My lungs closed up around the scream that threatened to escape as I felt his seed hit something deep inside me.

He took me down to the bed, his body hard, strong, pressing me down forcefully as he rode out the last of his orgasm and my body convulsed in the most earth shattering orgasms.

Chapter 11

LUCA

***

I woke up the next morning feeling better than I had in as long as I can remember. I waited for the dregs of the dream but it never came and then I remembered. I didn't need the dream. My eyes flew open and I looked down at the head that laid on my chest.

It was real; it was all real. I felt like someone who'd crashed after an extreme high, all the events of the previous day coming back full force. My heart felt…strange, almost complete, after living in darkness for so long.

The fire was low in the grate, the room warm and cozy. Outside the window, snow was falling and for the first time in a long-long time I felt the season in the air with something other than dread.

I massaged her scalp to wake her up before turning her onto her back. Last night, I'd had her too many times to count. My dick was raw and yet I wanted back inside her more than I needed my next breath. I had her on her back and was in her before her eyes were fully open on mine.

This loving was slow and tender, nothing like the night's madness, but it's what was needed. "Good morning wife." I buried my face in her neck and fucked into her nice and slow. Only our pelvises moved against each other as I tried to get my whole cock inside her. She was still too small, though her pussy had opened a little more during the night. "I'm going to have fun opening you up wide enough to take my cock."

She's so easy, the littlest things get her pussy juicing and my words were no different. "I love the way you respond to me. You're so passionate, so giving." I tasted the flesh of her neck between my teeth as she clamped down around me.

Her pussy was hot and tight. Just like the night before that combination had me close to the brink in a matter of minutes. That and the fact that I hadn't been inside anyone since the last time I had her four years ago.

She'd lost some of her shyness in the night. Now her hands roamed over my back, pulling me to her, her legs came around me beneath the sheets as I twisted my hips just enough to hit her sweet spot.

"Ohhh." Her nails dug into me as I sped up my thrusts and growled in her neck. I squeezed her just as I felt that sweet rush of release begin in my balls. "Yes...fuck." If not for our kids and the fact that my parents will be up soon and expecting us to put in an appearance I'd stay in her all day.

She was just as sweet as that first time. I'd done everything to her last night that I had our first night together. When her pussy got sore, I ate her to ease the pain. When she got too tired to ride my cock, I put her on her back and fucked her hard. But nothing beats when I take her from behind.

My thoughts had me racing towards completion.
"Are you close baby?" I needed her to be because every time I get into her my staying power becomes nil. "Cum for me Isabella." I pressed down on her clit and changed up my hip action, going at her from a different angle until my cock butted against that rough patch of flesh deep inside her continuously.

She really went off like a firecracker then. Her juices ran down my cock and onto the bed and her legs came up to wrap themselves higher around me as she clutched at me with her hands, pulling my head from her neck so she could push her tongue into my mouth. I'll have to remember that she likes to be kissed when she cums.

It felt like I emptied a gallon of jizz into her, which was surprising after how much I'd already cum inside her last night. "Uhhhhhh…" Something inside her triggered a second orgasm on top of the first and I went deaf dumb and blind for a hot minute.

"That was the one, that took all I had left. You've depleted me, now it's time for a shower and the kids then breakfast." The sun wasn't yet fully up but we had a full day ahead. I pulled her up from the bed and walked her naked to the en suite bathroom.

"You lost your tongue sweetheart?" She hadn't said one word since we woke up. "I'm processing." Well that was something. At least she wasn't running screaming from the house. But I wouldn't feel home free until I got the three of them on that plane and back to my place in New York. Speaking of which, I need to make some calls.

"And what's your verdict?" I ran my soapy hands over her front as her back rested against my chest. "Open." She opened her legs to give me free rein and I washed her pussy clean of our juices before letting the water wash the soap away. I wrapped my hand around her neck and pulled her head back so I could reach her mouth and feed her my tongue.

With one hand on her flat tummy, I pulled her ass back into me and slid home. "I'm going to do you rough this time." She lifted up on her toes as I pushed my fat cock deep into her belly. Using the hand around her neck and the one on her stomach I pulled her on and off my cock, pounding in and out of her as the water ran down on us.

"Fuck how is your pussy so good?" And she was, the best and that fucked with my head. What if I'd never found her, found them? "All those years, just the memory of this…" She moaned out loud no longer silent. "That's it baby you can scream as loud as you want to in here. Scream for me. Tell me what I want to hear."

"Fuck me Luca." I slammed into her and she came all over my cock. Thrashing and fucking back at me as I fucked her like a wild man. "Shit, fuck." I stumbled back as I came hard and held her tight to me.

Our hearts raced together as we fought to come back to earth. "Damn Isabella." I had to work my way out of her since she still had a tight lock on my cock, which refused to go down. "Let's see how well you learned last night."

I helped her to her knees and threw my head back as she took my cock hungrily into her mouth. She made the sexiest fucking noises as she sucked her juices and mine from my cock as the warm water ran down on her hair and back.

"Oh yeah, quick learner." I pumped in and out of her mouth slowly until I hit the back of her neck and she gagged. "Do that again." She did and my toes curled as I grabbed fistfuls of her hair.

"Enough." I pulled her off my cock and pushed her back against the wall, slamming into her so hard I was afraid I'd hurt her.

"Shit, sorry baby, shh." She wrapped her arms around my head and held on as I fucked her like I hadn't been inside her for the last ten hours give or take. It was as though we were both trying to make up for lost time. "Mouth." I pushed my tongue past her lips as something unfurled in my chest. Something deep, and powerful, that I had no name for.

"Cum on my cock, come on baby cum for me again." Her nipple in my mouth helped her along and she flooded my cock with her sweet essence once more, but I was still not even close.

"I need you flat on your back." I stumbled out of the shower stall with her in my arms and took her down to the plush sheepskin mat still stroking into her.

Her legs went up around my shoulders, opening her up even more. "That's right baby give me that pussy." She fucked herself ferociously on my cock as I plowed in and out of her. I bit and sucked every bit of her flesh I could reach as I raced towards another climax.

"Say the words."

"Fuck me Luca." This time she whispered the words sultrily in my ear and that's all it took. I fucked the first few jets into her and then stopped, holding still so that I could enjoy the pulsing of her pussy around my cock as the last drops of my seed spilled into her.

We shared an intimate kiss, our mouths mating as we ground out the last of an earthshattering climax together.

A quick shower followed and then it was time to get dressed and go see about the kids. I looked at her clothes for the first time while we got dressed. Yesterday I hadn't really noticed them under that ugly coat that I was going to burn first chance I get. "Get a move on Mrs. Deleon, we have a full day ahead of us."

"Oh crap mom." She rushed around the bed for her purse and grabbed her phone. "Oh shoot it's dead." She looked around the room I guess for a charger. "What kind of phone do you have?" I went to get mine from the drawer where I'd dropped it on arrival. She named some off brand thing that I was sure I'd never heard of before.

"I have an iPhone sorry. Just use this to call." I passed her my phone and went into the closet for something to wear. I came back into the room to hushed tones as she tried to explain things to her mom and not very successfully from her end.

"Mom, I'll tell you every…" I took the phone from her hand and picked up the conversation. "Hello Mrs. Clifton, this is Luca, your daughter and I have a lot to tell you so why don't you take down this address? We'll be out most of the day but six o'clock this evening should be good. I'll see you then."

I hung up and fielded her wrath as was to be expected. "Are you crazy she's probably freaking out and my phone is dead so she can't reach me." She's actually pretty cute when she gets pissed. "Calm down babe, she got it once I told her my name. Now unless I miss my guess our kids will be up soon and we don't want them waking up in a strange place without one of us there."

She fussed the whole time she got dressed in the same clothes from yesterday. I knew what we were doing first today. We walked down the hall together and I could hear my parents moving around downstairs with the servants.

I opened the door to the nursery and all the love and emotion I'd felt the day before came rushing back tenfold. They were here, safe, my kids. I felt a tinge of fear mixed in with the love and forced it back. Last time I wasn't there, I didn't keep him safe. Now I had two and there was nothing I wouldn't do to keep them safe and happy.

This was my second chance, my own Christmas miracle. It's been a while since I've believed in such things. Yesterday when I rushed her into marriage I hadn't thought of the future and what a life together would be. But after last night, dare I hope? Better not tempt fate.

My son had left his bed and was now cuddled up with his sister, protecting her, his little arm around her. It was so much something I would do that it left me choked up. How could they have so much of me in them? I look at them in the little time we've had together and see so much of the boy I used to be.

"He does that sometimes." She came to stand next to me by the bed. "They're tired poor things. Usually they'd have been up by now. We have to get them up, I have work."

"Not today you don't."
"Excuse me I need that job."
"Do you? And how do you plan on doing it from New York?" She didn't have a ready comeback but I was sure she'd come up with something soon enough.

Just then the door opened behind us and ma came in. "Oh, are they awake?" She whispered as she snuck her way in. "Isn't that adorable? You used to do the same thing. I'd wake in the morning and you'd have left your room and crawled in with Susie." She had tears in her eyes.

"Breakfast is ready you two. Why don't you go on ahead and I'll stay up here with these two? I found some things of their cousins that they can wear for today."

"Thanks ma, I've got it covered. After breakfast we're going shopping." I led Isabella from the room before she could argue. "By the way ma expect company this evening. Isabella's parents will be here around six."

"No problem son, just tell Aggie there'll be two more for dinner." She'd already forgotten all about me before the door closed. That was something else I had to be grateful for, giving ma her grandkids. No matter how many she has there's never enough. My younger siblings have given her more than enough to keep her busy, but I never heard the end of the baby plea.

When little Sam had died in that crash it had gutted all of us. He was the first grandchild by a few months, and my parents had been so proud. Ma still had a million pictures of him around the house and yesterday it was still a little hard to see him, especially at this time. But that pain had been eased just a little.

I didn't miss the fact that she had come to me pretty much by the same way I'd lost them. It was a patch of ice that had destroyed the life I had, and now it looks like it was the same that had given me a new one.

"Don't be nervous baby, it's just breakfast." I took her to the dining room where the breakfast buffet was already set up. She was looking around as if expecting someone to ask her to leave. The house kinda has that effect on people.

"Have a seat, I'll fix you a plate." For once she obeyed without question. I filled both our plates with some of everything as the Christmas music that usually made me crazy played cheerily in the background.

This morning I welcomed it, along with the new outlook on life. "Momma, mommy." I grinned as the two of them ran into the room at full speed. "Do they always do that? Call your name one after the other like that?"

"It's a competition. Your daughter can't let her brother one up her in anything. He on the other hand always takes a step back and lets her lead." I watched as they rushed her and I got a front row seat to what it was going to be like to wake up with my family every morning.

They finally turned their attention to me and my little guy went shy while his sister smiled and flirted. Well damn, I see private school in her future. She batted her lashes and held her arms out to be held and daddy melted.

"How did you sleep princess?" I had time to kiss her little head before she was off and running again. Her mother was tense and watched them both like a hawk. "Relax baby, I've broken lots of shi…stuff in here and I'm still alive to tell it."

Her smile didn't quite reach her eyes but at least she wasn't looking ready to bolt.

"Are you two ready for breakfast?" I got up to go fix them each a plate not sure what kids their age ate. She must've seen my confusion because she came to the rescue. "They can eat pretty much the same things we do but smaller portions." She rolled her eyes at me. I guess I'd fed her too much.

The breakfast table was noisier than it had been since my siblings and I were kids. It was beautiful. Ma joined us soon after with dad in tow. "We'll just have coffee dears we've already eaten."

They hogged the kids and I could already see where this was going. Ma had Luna on her lap and dad took Luca. "Why don't we keep the kids here while you two go shopping?"

"Perfect." I'd planned to take them with us but remembering the absolute excitement and joy of opening presents under the tree I wanted that for them. I wanted to see the looks of surprise and glee on their faces when they tore into that paper tomorrow morning. Plus my wife needed a complete new wardrobe and that could take a while.

"I don't think…" I squeezed her hand where it laid on the table. "They'll be fine babe." I could see how hard it was for her to give in. She must feel like she was losing control of her life, but she had to accept that there were other people in our children's lives now, that she didn't have to do it alone.

"I have to call my job and tell them I'm not coming in." She excused herself from the room once ma directed her to the nearest phone. Poor thing, I think she's still shell shocked. It'll only get worse before the holiday was over. I was in the mood to spoil them.

She came back and it was time to go. Ma bribed the kids with a trip to the stables out back and we were soon easily forgotten. It was the parents who had a hard time leaving. I didn't expect to feel this strong a pull so soon, but walking out the door with their gleeful laughter following me was hard.

"You call your boss?"
"Yeah."
"You tell him you're quitting?" "No."
"Why not?"

"Because, I don't know. This doesn't feel real yet I guess. What if I give up everything and follow you to New York and hate it? Or you change your mind? It's not easy raising two kids you know. Sure it's all fun and games now because you just met them. But you haven't dealt with being up all night when they're both sick and wanting your attention and…"

"Hey, not my fault that I wasn't there, so don't go there. Second, you're gonna love New York and it's not like you'll be a million miles away we can come back as often as you like. And last but not least you don't have a choice. So whenever you start feeling like you are right now, just tell yourself that it's all on me. The man who wants to take you and our children out of the borderline poverty in which you now exist and give you something better."

I put the SUV in drive and stopped myself from peeling out of there. Snow was coming down to join the few inches that had already fallen. No way was I going to risk our lives by being stupid just because she was pissing me off.

I didn't have to go all the way to Manchester since the shops I was looking for were closer to home. Though New York would be better, this would do for now. She didn't say anything to me all the way there and I left her to her sulk.

I guess it was too much to ask that a night of hot fucking would thaw her contrary ass a bit. Whatever! As long as her ass was on that plane in a few days, she could bitch all she wanted for now.

She found her voice when we stopped in at the first shop. "What're we doing here? I thought you were getting toys for the kids?" She was still pissy, too bad. She wasn't about to ruin my mood. This was the first Christmas I'd looked forward to in four years. I have a hell of a lot to be thankful for, including her ass, and that's where I'm at.

"You, don't say anything unless you have something useful to say." A sales lady saw us and came over. I told her what I wanted, she eyeballed Isabella and we followed her into the store while she gave us a running marathon speech of all the new things they'd just got into the store that would be just perfect for her.

I hadn't missed the look she'd given Isabella, or the distinction she'd made between the differences in our clothes. I pulled my phone and called ma. She answered and I could hear the twins' gibberish and the neighing of horses in the background.

"They're fine son, I did raise four of you-you know."
"Thanks ma, but that's not why I'm calling. I need you to call your lady, you know, the one that turns your scary mess into the belle of the ball?"

"Excuse me, but I'll have you know Sylvia says I'm her easiest client. She hardly has to do anything with me."
"Sure and I'm the king of France."
"France doesn't have a king son."
"Exactly."

"Oh you hush. I'll call her what time do you want her here?"

"Four-ish."

"Will do." I hung up and went to oversee whatever those two were doing. All I'd seen while I was on the phone was a lot of head shaking from Isabella and it usually came after she'd seen the price tag. "We'll take this one in the black and tan." I pointed out the Vee-necked cashmere sweater to the sales lady before moving down the table.

Isabella opened her mouth to object but all it took was a look to shut her down. I chose four more sweaters, a couple turtlenecks and some suede slacks and leggings. "Let's go." I took her hand in one of mine, and the bags with her loot in the other.

Our next stop was the shoe store where I got her a couple pairs of boots but since I wasn't too jazzed about their collection I stopped there. She balked at the entrance to the lingerie store but I dragged her in and chose whatever I liked, all the while imagining tearing them off of her.

I had to damn near hogtie her when I got her the new full- length shearling with fox lining. "Okay, that's it for today. We'll have lunch then hit the kid's stores." We were loaded down so we made a quick trip back to the truck before heading to the food court. We both settled for hot chocolate with whip cream and warm freshly baked raspberry croissants.

I found us a table that allowed us some privacy. Since she was being a good girl and not giving me any shit, I decided to make another necessary call. "Tory, it's me. I need a favor." "It's Christmas Luca for crap sake take a break."

"Tory, your holiday is over don't give me any crap."
"Okay-okay what is it that you want? It better not involve me going out in this fuckery that's going on outside. It's cold as balls."

"I need you to turn one of the extra bedrooms, the one closest to the master into a nursery for toddlers."

"What the hell? You fall and hit your head or something?" "I'll tell you all about it when we get home. They're three years old, one of each, so I need the room done up to suit. One side for a princess the other for a prince." I took the phone away from my ear for a second.

"What's the name of those things the kids like again?"
"Hello Kitty and Ninja Turtles." I passed on the information. "It would be really great if you can have that started by the time we get home next week. Oh, and that big stuffed bear they have every year in the window of FAO Swartz, work that in there somewhere. Thanks love, I owe you one."

"Love? You've really hit your head. Who the hell is this? And what did you do with the ornery puissant, Luca Deleon?" "Smartass." I hung up and caught the look on my wife's face. "Problem?"

"I don't want one of your women buying things for my kids." Ooh, jealousy. I like it. I grinned and picked up my cup. "Tory is sixty if she's a day." "So, what does that mean? Haven't you heard about cougars?"

"That maybe but I don't think her hulk of a husband would approve." She sure is a funny one. She pretends not to care, not to want me, other than my dick that is, but she's jealous of a phone call.

"I'm no cheat sweetheart, that's one thing you never have to worry about. I don't have to tell you what I'd do to you if you ever betrayed our vows, so let's just say on that score we're clear."

"How do I know you're telling me the truth? How do I know that you're not going to take me there away from everything and everyone I know and then turn into some playboy womanizing abuser?"

'That night, the first night we met. You saw me at my worse. Did I abuse you then? Since we met yesterday, when I found out that you've had my kids for three years without even trying to find me, did I strangle the shit out of you? No? Well then, I guess you can put that shit out of your head."

She was biting her tongue. I could tell by the way she held her mouth. "Don't do that, you have something to say, say it." She tore apart that croissant like it was the enemy.

"Don't you find this whole thing crazy?"

"We've already had this conversation. Yesterday, before I had you, again, I would've said I'll take my kids and you can stay here since you seem so attached. But now there isn't a snowball's chance in hell that I'm leaving any of you behind. The best thing you can do instead of imagining every worse case scenario there is, is try to look at the bright side. You just married a man who's worth millions. Your children now have a father, not to mention aunts and uncles and grandparents who would give their life to save theirs. What exactly do you find wrong with that?"

"I don't want you to take over." She said it so low I had to ask her to repeat herself and when she did I finally got it-Sort of. "You come from this amazing family and you have all this money like you said. What do I have? What's to stop you from trying to take them from me?" I took my time answering, because contrary to what she believed I did understand how hard this was for her.

Only in fairytales do women just run off into the sunset with the strange man, who knocked them up and then disappeared, only to return years later and sweep them off their feet.

"I'm asking you to trust me. You saw what happened last night. Trust me, if I wanted to take the kids or make life hard for you, all it would've taken is one phone call. My uncle isn't only good for getting rushed marriage license. Look I told you, our kids deserve the life I can give them. You deserve it. It couldn't have been easy going it alone. Tell me about it."

"It wasn't as bad as all that. Not once I got past the fear and panic. My parents were a huge help. I guess the hardest part was having to drop out of school. I could've continued for another semester while I was pregnant, but I needed the money for the babies."

"What were you studying?" I hated to interrupt. I hadn't realized after she started talking how much I wanted to know about that time in her life. I wanted to know everything I'd missed. When Abigail was pregnant with Sam it was a family affair, everyone was involved.

I hated that I'd missed it all with her and the twins. In my family being a dad doesn't just start once the baby's born. We're more hands on. I felt Sam kick, got to see him grow…

"Law. I wanted to be a lawyer. But after the babies, that wasn't plausible. Mom and dad helped me go to school to get my paralegal certificate. They've been there every step of the way. Mom is a great help with babysitting. She watches the twins when I have to go to work, that helps with childcare."

She stopped to take a sip of her chocolate while I took it all in. I looked around at all the people going about their day. Enjoying for the first time in four years the sights and sounds of joy that the holiday season brings.

Even the smell of something sweet with a hint of cinnamon baking that wafted through the air added a little… something to the ambience. But most of all, it was my new family that I was looking forward to spending this time with.

"Thank you."
"For what?" She seemed actually stymied.
"For what? For all the things you just mentioned. For having my kids when let's face it, you didn't have to."

"Oh, there was never any question that I would have them. Of course I cursed you a thousand times when I was hung over the bowl being sick as a dog. But not once did I think of not having the baby. Then when I found out there was going to be two of them I thought for sure I was going to lose it."

She smiled as she said it but I could only imagine the fear. I listened to her tell cute little stories about her cumbersome girth once she got too big to even tie her shoes. I remember going through that with my first wife, something else I had missed.

As I sat there listening, watching, I realized I liked her. She was amazingly smart, beautiful with a heart of gold. I got all of that from the way she'd handled herself the last four years. From the fact that she wasn't even remotely interested in my money.

"What?" She looked at me questioningly.
"What-what?" She did that thing where she tries to hide behind her hair and I couldn't resist reaching across the table to push it back behind her ear. "Tell me." She shrugged her shoulders and played with her pastry. "You were staring."

"I was just admiring my wife. You know there's another side to this that you haven't given much thought to."
"What's that?"

"I have just as much reason to be leery of you as you do me. For all I know, you could be some kind of crazy nut who's going to turn my life upside down. I just married you and I have no idea who you really are. I did it for the most obvious reason, our children, but like I've already told you. It's best to find the silver lining because there's nowhere to go but forward. Come on let's go spoil our kids."

Chapter 12

BELLA

***

And spoil them he did. "Luca that's way too much." He bought out the better part of two toy stores and I don't even want to start on clothes. "What are they going to do with all this stuff?" This was beyond me.

On the one hand, I was excited that my kids were going to have something more than the few paltry plastic toys I had already bought, and had hidden at mom and dad's. And then there was the side of me that was worried about them really becoming spoilt.

"Babe you worry too much. Every kid should have a million toys under the tree come Christmas day. My parents did the same for me and I turned out ok." Boy did he ever. All day I've been watching him. Watching to see when that façade would crack, when the real him would show up.

I couldn't believe that he really was this person. This selfless man who one day finds out he's a father and without a thought for himself beyond being a part of his children's lives would do all that he had done.

I guess he has a point. I could very well be a loose canon, how was he to know? I'm as much a stranger to him as he is to me. But I'm afraid I knew what the problem was. I wanted him to want me and I'm not just talking sex. Obviously we had no issues there. But all he keeps talking about is the kids. And I feel like a monster for even thinking this way.

I should be jumping for joy that this man who had so much to offer my kids, who has shown so far that he truly does care for them, wants them in his life. Instead, I'm secretly begrudging the fact that he's doesn't seem to want me as much.

"Why have you gone so quiet all of a sudden?" We were driving back to his parents. I hadn't realized there was a lull in the conversation once I got lost in my head. "No reason. I was just thinking about the kids." Liar.

We unpacked the SUV with help from his dad, who like his son, seemed very accepting of having a ready made family fall in his lap two days before the holiday. "How was your day Bella?"

"It was fun thank you."
"Well come on in here, Connie has some warm cider waiting and I think there's someone waiting here for you." I looked at my watch and then back at Luca. It was too early for my parents; maybe it was one of his family members.

"I forgot all about that, sorry sweetheart. You'll meet her soon enough." Very cryptic but then again I had come to learn that Luca only said as much as he needed to. Inside, there was a very stylish woman sitting with Luca's mom, Connie having Cider.

"Oh hello dear, this is Sylvia she works wonders, we have you all set up in the salon." She was talking too fast for her words to make sense and before I knew it I was being dragged off to the back of the house.

"Wait." Luca caught up with me and I was almost relieved to be saved from whatever this was but it was short lived. "It'll be fine sweetheart, I'm right out here."

"But I didn't get to see the kids."
"Oh, they're having their nap dear. All that fussing around in the stables tired them out poor things. I think you're going to have a time on your hands in New York. They loved the horses. Maybe that would be incentive enough for you to move back home. There's no better place to raise children." And with that I was rushed off and away about to face who knows what.

Chapter 13

LUCA

***

I took the stairs two at a time leaving dad and Aggie and the rest of the staff to drag the toys into the den for later. I opened the door to the nursery and wondered how long it would be before this feeling disappeared. How long before I no longer get choked up at the sight of them.

There's so much I have to do. Most of it will have to wait because of the holiday, but as soon as we get back to New York I had a whole list of things that needed doing for my family.

Luna's little arm would look perfect with a bracelet but where would I hide Luca's tracker? Boys weren't big on bracelets and he was too young for a watch. Maybe, I'll get him something that I have, something that he'd be proud to wear because his daddy has one too.

Their mother's was easy. I'll put hers in something she was sure never to remove. "Shit, I need to get her a ring." For some reason the thought of placing such a public statement of ownership on her hand made my heart beat wildly in my chest.

I sat in there with the kids for a few minutes just sucking in the joy. The season didn't suck as much as it had in the past. In fact, I couldn't wait for tomorrow, to see the looks on my children's faces.

There are no words to describe what I felt as I sat there looking at them. Alone with my thoughts for the first time, I let it all sink in. This was my life. The change had come out of nowhere and was totally unexpected, but no less appreciated.

I shed a tear for my dead son and his mother. I don't think I will ever fully say goodbye to them, how can I? They were once a big part of my life and there will always be a place for them in my heart. But this, these two and the woman downstairs who I'd just thrown to the wolves. They were my future.

I got up from my seat on the bottom bunk and walked over to the bed where they both laid sleeping. Life truly is stranger than fiction. I suffered my greatest loss because of this holiday four years ago. At least that's how I'd always seen it in my head. Had Abigail not gone shopping they would still be alive.

I've hated this time of year and especially Christmas day since then. Now life had given back twice over. They were conceived the night before Christmas, and I found them two days before. Looks like my moratorium against all things Christmas was over.

On that thought, I headed back downstairs to get started on wrapping the mountain of gifts we'd got them. She's right, I may have gone a little overboard, but who can blame me? I had three years to make up for and it looks like I'd got a good head start. It would be nothing to pack them all up for home so I wasn't worried.

I was in there, ten minutes sorting things out when dad came in. "Are you here to help wrap?" We both hated giftwrapping I remember, but this time it didn't feel as much of a chore as it did a pleasure.

"I can but that's not why I'm here." He was holding something in his hand and for one of the few times in my life he seemed uncertain of himself. "What you got there, dad?" I kept turning the box with the three- foot doll over in my hand to figure out where to start.

"Well, son, last time you got married your wife wanted a more modern ring. I was hoping this time my new daughter might like a piece of our family history…" I stopped and looked at him.

"Great-great grandma's ring." He was right, Abigail had her own style and it was certainly nothing against her that she'd chosen a more up to date design. She hadn't rejected the family heirloom in fact she'd never seen it. But she'd shown me the ring she'd always wanted and that's the one she'd got.

He held the little antique box out to me with a slight tremble in his hand. It had been years since I'd seen the ring. It was a beauty to be sure. A single stone on a bed of gold filigree. It would be almost too simple if not for the artwork and the three and a half carat diamond.

"You can have it reset if you'd like or whatever."

"No dad it's perfect, it's her." And it was. It had that same old world beauty she does. Strong, classic, beautiful. "Thanks dad." He rubbed my shoulder before taking a seat across from me.

"Now, let's see if we can get through this lot before Christmas. I'm very proud of you son." He was looking at a box with one of Luca's toys in it with a confused look on his face.

"Why?"

"Because of the way you've handled this situation. Not many men would've done it the same. Especially a man in your position. They would've asked for DNA and any other kind of proof they could."

"Dad all you have to do is look at them to see they're mine."

"I know it, good grief it was like being sent back in time. And they have so much of you in them son." He smiled fondly as he figured out the box in his hand and where to start. Nobody made just plain square boxes anymore.

"Your mother and I took them down to the stables and had a hell of a time on our hands keeping them from climbing the horses. And that little miss, you're gonna have your hands full. She wanted to know why she couldn't ride the horsey and when we took them down to the pond she almost jumped right in. Just like you remember? And your son, the way he stands back and lets her run the show but always with a watchful eye making sure she's safe." He shook his head.

"Damn if I haven't seen you do that same thing with your siblings a thousand times. I tell you it's the best. I have one grievance with you though."

"Yeah, and what's that?"

"Well, why do you always have to show me up with your mother?"

"I don't follow." I waited for his answer as he wrestled with the gigantic roll of giftwrap paper. "Well you know how she's always wanted to sail around the world. Well I finally made all the preparations. Hired a crew to man the yacht and take us wherever her little heart desires. Your brother was going to fill in for the year hiatus I planned to take."

"I don't see how I've shown you up. You don't even know what I got her."

"Are you kidding me? Two grandbabies days before Christmas? Who the hell can top that? Not to mention it would take a stick of dynamite to get her on that fool boat now. I'm already expecting having to spend every damn weekend in that damn city you up and moved to."

"Sorry dad. Better luck next year." He had a point and we both knew he was right. No way was ma going to go anywhere. I was already dreading the leave in the next few days because I knew she was going to cry and plead with me like she always do to stay a little longer, to come home.

I put the ring in my pocket and got back to work, already imagining just how I was going to put it on her finger. Now I couldn't wait for the night to be over so I could do just that.

It felt like hours had passed when I heard the kids' voices. Aggie was telling them about snacks and their little squeals of delight were music to my ears and a song in my heart. "Break time." Dad had helped me plow through the mountain of gifts and we were both easing out the kinks as we stood to our feet for the first time since entering the room.

I found them in the kitchen getting ready to be strapped into the seats my parents had attached to a little breakfast bar they kept for the grandkids. "Daddy." I stopped dead in my tracks when my daughter ran to me with outstretched arms. Dad clapped me on the shoulder once it was obvious that I couldn't move.

"Hi princess." I picked her up and hugged her too tight, I was sure, as her brother true to form stood back and waited his turn. I got to my knees and opened my other arm for him and pulled him into our little family hug. How did they know? Isabella and I hadn't even gotten around to discussing how we were going to break the news to them.

She came into the room with ma on her heels and I looked up at her. She looked amazing. Her beautiful hair now had a healthy shine and the fat curls she'd had balled on top of her head now fell to the middle of her back. "You look beautiful." She smiled shyly and ran her hand over her hair and down over the new outfit she'd changed into that fit her perfectly.

"My parents will be here any minute." Shit, I'd almost forgot. "You told them?" I looked at the kids so she'd know what I was talking about. "They asked. Well to be exact your daughter asked." She looked nervous as she said it.

"Thank you." I didn't realize how quiet all the adults in the room including Aggie had gone during this exchange. Then ma started talking and the spell was broken.

"Aggie is everything ready? Our guests should be arriving soon." Ma was moving around the room like a crazy person fixing the already perfect house. "So what's the plan? What did you and your family have planned for tonight?"

"Well, we were going to have dinner, and then once the kids were in bed we were going to wrap their gifts and put them under the tree. That's about it. You don't have to change anything; we'll do whatever your parents are accustomed to. I don't want to make any trouble."

"Trust me, there's nothing you could possibly do to cause trouble. Look at them." Ma and dad were showing the kids all the family ornaments we'd collected over the years. Some of them were over a hundred years old. "We have a tradition in the family, every year the kids get their own ornament for the tree. We started a bit late this year, but definitely next year we'll get on that."

"Okay." I could see she was getting nervous again but couldn't figure why. And when the doorbell rang announcing her parents, she almost jumped out of her skin. We'd got her a new charger for her phone so I was sure she must've found time to call her mom by now.

I walked with her to the door behind Aggie as she answered it. The couple standing there were probably a few years younger than my parents. I could see the resemblance right off; she had her mother's eyes and hair.

"Mom, dad you made it." She hugged them and I shook hands under very intense stares before we walked them into the living room where my parents were waiting to meet them. Introductions were made and drinks passed around. I stuck close to her because she seemed overly nervous. "Where's Melissa?"

"Oh, we decided that it was best if she met everyone another time." Her body relaxed visibly at that and I wondered who this Melissa was and why she made my wife so tense.

The evening as far as I could tell was a success. No one was crass enough to come right out and mention how we'd met and how our kids had come to be, though I was sure she'd given her parents a watered down version same as I'd done with mine.

In the midst of all the revelry, while both sets of grandparents were focused on the kids, I pulled her aside. "What did you tell them about us?"

"They knew the story a long time ago when I showed up pregnant. I told them that we met and uh had a very short relationship and you were gone long before I knew I was pregnant." Close enough to the one I'd told.

As the evening wore on, things got a lot more relaxed among the families. Her parents were a bit tense in the beginning but my ancestral home usually has that affect on first time visitors. But it wasn't long before the warmth of the fireplace, the twinkling lights on the ten foot tree, and the soft strings of the Christmas carols in the background had everyone relaxed and at ease.

And of course the children were the center of attention, and they loved it. We hadn't put their gifts under the tree yet, that was for later. But ma, the wonder woman had already hung stockings with their names and their grandma Clifton had brought some as well.

It was amazing to watch their innocence and the absolute joy they had in things I'd long taken for granted. When they were through exploring the tree and shaking the gifts while laughing, they just sat there and watched the lights twinkle on and off, talking to each other in their special language. It was perfect.

Ma was her usual friendly self and I could see she was going out of her way to impress my new in-laws. Though I did sense a little bit of friendly rivalry between the grandmothers. Whenever one of the kids ran to Ellen, Isabella's mom, ma would get this look on her face. Not like she was displeased, but I could tell the fact that the other woman had a closer relationship with the kids was a little bit hard for her.

She'd missed so much, we all had. But I had no doubt we'd make up for it, starting now. "Hey kids how would you like to go play in the snow with daddy?"

"Luca, it's almost their bedtime." The kids were already squealing and running for the door while my wife griped at me. I wrapped an arm around her shoulder and pulled her along with me.

"All the better. This way they will be too tired to stay up and then daddy can take mommy to bed and celebrate their anniversary." I looked at my watch. "Which should be in about three hours." I whispered the words so only she could hear, but I'm sure her blush gave everyone else a good idea what I'd just said to her.

"Hold it." I caught up with the kids at the door and grabbed their new snowsuits from the closet. Isabella joined me in putting their suits on and then the whole family got bundled up and headed outside so I could have my first snowball fight with my kids.

"Daddy-daddy, do me." That's my little princess. I was swinging her brother around by the arms making him giggle uproariously while she built a snowman with her mom and grandmothers. The men had gone off so dad could show Nigel, her dad, something in his little hobby shed.

"Okay princess come." I kissed my boy and dropped one of his hands and took one of Luna's so she could have some of the same. Somehow the three of us ended up rolling around in the snow. I felt a splash of cold hit me square in the back of the head and looked around to see my wife running away.

"Sneaky. Come on kids let's get mommy."
"No, Luca it's too cold." She ran laughing and tried to hide behind her mom and mine. I hefted the snowball in my hand and looked at the three of them. "You'd better not." She was laughing too hard to talk straight.

I let fly with the snowball and all three of them got a piece of it. "This means war, come on ladies let's get him." That's my ma. The kids and I had a battle on our hands and these women were vicious. I ended up on the ground more than anything since my kids were like snow bunnies.

"Daddy loves you both very much." We'd been rolling around and they were both out of breath. I looked down at them with all the wonder of snow and Christmas lights, and ma's million and one decorations hanging from every door and window and the love just hit me in the gut like a fastball.

"Love you too, daddy."

"Me too daddy." I got covered with the most precious kisses and hugs then. Ma brought out a tray of chocolate and cookies for everyone and the men were on their way back by then. They both had a good laugh at the rest of us with our snow covered hats and red cheeks.

It was the most magical Christmas Eve I'd had in four years. And I planned on making it even better. I patted my pocket where I'd put her ring earlier just to be sure it was still there. "I think that's a wonderful idea."

"What's a wonderful idea ma?" She looked more alive than I'd seen her in a long time as I put my arm around her shoulders and kissed her hair.

"Your dad has invited the Ellen and Nigel to join us tomorrow. Isn't that lovely? Come on kids let grandmas get you ready for bed. You two look wiped. Honey, why don't you offer Nigel some of that nice cognac you have?"

"I did love but he declined, they're driving back and the roads aren't the best."
"Of course what was I thinking? I wish I'd have thought to tell you to pack an overnight bag, that way you wouldn't have to go out in that and then make the trek again tomorrow."

"Oh, that's perfectly alright. Our younger daughter will be home any minute and we promised we'd be there."

"Oh well, why didn't you bring her along? We would've been happy to have her."

"She had...other plans." I didn't like the look that passed between her and my wife when she said that and I got the feeling I was missing something really important. I soon forgot all about it in the midst of squeals and giggles as they tried to take my kids up for their baths.

My siblings called, it seems ma had called them with the news and now they were upset that they weren't here to meet my new family. The three of them and their families had taken a trip to Paris for the holiday and wouldn't be back until after the New Year.

We made plans to meet up in New York and instead of the pitying condolences I always dreaded, I got congratulations. I had to promise Susie that I'd send her some of the pictures I'd snapped before she'd get off the phone.

Chapter 14

LUCA

***

By the time Isabella's parents left, it was coming on to the magic hour. My body was already preparing, not that I haven't been in a constant state of semi-arousal since yesterday.

After the kids were settled and the house was quiet, I hustled her off to bed. "I'll light the fire and grab a quick shower." I leaned over her for a kiss as she sat in the chair removing her boots.

I took the shortest shower in history before drying off and rushing back to her. "Oh damn." She'd changed into one of the silk negligees she'd fought so hard against me buying.

It was champagne colored with pale pink lace edging and barely reached above her knees. It wasn't the color I was interested in though, but the way the soft silk contoured her body.

Her breasts were nicely rounded, her tummy concave and her hips and ass, wow. I dropped the towel as I walked over to her before the fire where she'd been warming herself. I'd put the ring in the nightstand when she wasn't looking. I had a great of idea of how and when I wanted to give it to her.

Now I pulled her to me with a hand behind her head and covered her lips with mine. I wrapped an arm around her, pulling her silk clad body in close so that my cock slid into the vee between her thighs.

"Umm, you feel so good." I slid my hand under the nightie and up between her thighs as I tongue fucked her mouth and drove my fingers inside her already wet pussy. "You're ready for me, I like that."

She moaned into my mouth and rode my fingers as I went after her clit with my thumb. "I was going to take you to bed and make love to you. Maybe later. I'm going to mount you here before the fire first."

I took her down to the rug, just like I had in that other place, four years ago. Pushing the silk up above her navel, I took the time to admire her freshly shaved pussy before spreading her open for my tongue.

I lifted her ass like an offering in my hands and brought her to my mouth. Her smoothness brushed against my lips as I licked her folds before letting my tongue slip inside her for a taste.

My eyes closed as her taste rushed into me, and when her hands came down to hold my head in place between her widespread legs my heart rate sky-rocketed.

She moved against my mouth as I sunk my tongue deep into her, sucking her juices as I stroked my leaking cock to readiness. Images of all I would do to her played behind my closed lids and I was soon turning her onto her hands and knees.

I slapped her pussy with my cock and her ass jumped but I wasn't ready to fuck. I wanted her mindless with need before I gave her what she wanted. What we both needed.

"Who's my bad girl?" she looked over her shoulder in surprise and her face went up in flames but she answered. "Me."
"And what does my bad girl want?" I gave her my mouth making it hard for her to answer as I ate her from behind.

Holding her hips between my hands, I tongued her pussy until her juices filled my mouth. I teased her tight little rosebud with the tip of my thumb before easing it in and she spread wider for me.

"Fuck me Luca." The magic words. I rose up behind her and slammed my cock into her pink gash and she screamed. Covering her mouth with my hand, I rode high and deep, forcing more of my cock into her than I ever had before.

She arched her back and I slipped in deeper. "That's it, cock that ass for me baby. Look how good you're taking me!" I felt tears hit the hand that I had over her mouth.

"Shh, the pain will ease soon I promise. I'm almost all the way inside you." She nodded as I wrapped my free hand around her middle, using it to pull her back onto my cock.

Her pussy clenched and gushed juice all over my cock so I knew she was enjoying what I was doing to her. I moved my hand down to her clit and pressed and she opened up a little bit more.

"Oh yeah, that's it." I eased out nice and slow and slid back in, taking my time as I fucked into her at a steady pace, doing my best to open her up with my girth. Her pussy stretched over my cock like a thick layer of skin and the sight of it enticed me to madness. "Hang on!"

She bit into my hand hard when I started pile driving into her upturned pink hole. I was deeper in her than I'd ever been, my whole dick disappearing with each stroke. Her ass shook and she came, clamping down on my dick like a vise.

Her arms gave out and her body dropped to the floor but I wasn't done. I held her hips in my hands keeping her ass in the air so could fuck as deep, as hard as I wanted. When I came this time, I put it in her womb and held still until I was dry.

When I could feel my legs again, I lifted her and took her to bed for more of the same. I gave her my mouth again tasting both our juices but I didn't care. The night had turned into something wild and undisciplined.

Her body was perfect; she was perfect. The way she responded, the wild sounds she made went straight to my heart. And as I slid up her body after bringing her off with my mouth, and slipped into her sweet slippery heat, I let her into my heart.

We looked into each other's eyes as I laid on top of her, my cock thumping along with my heartbeat. "You're beautiful you know that." She blushed and bit into her lip.

I moved a lock of hair back off her forehead and kissed her lightly there before reaching over to the nightstand. "Close your eyes sweetheart." I waited until she obeyed before opening the box and retrieving the ring.

"Open." I took her hand and slipped the ring on her finger. "This never comes off no matter what." I kissed her finger before bringing both our hands to my heart.

Her eyes filled up with tears. "Shh it's okay Isabella, everything's going to be okay from now on I promise. I'm going to take very good care of you." That only seemed to make her cry harder so I hugged her closer and turned us on our sides with my cock still buried inside her.

I spoke softly to her as I ran my hand up and down her back soothingly with her head on my chest. "There's nothing for you to be afraid of anymore baby. This." I picked up the hand with my ring on it.

"Means that you're mine, you're part of me. I will always watch over you. Haven't you been happy these last two days? Don't you like me even a little bit?"

"Of course I like you. I…" She stopped and buried her face in my chest and held on tight. "You what baby?" She took her time answering while I held her close to my heart.

"I've been in love with a memory for a long time. And now you're here and I'm scared."

"What are you afraid of?" She started to shake and I had to wrap my leg around her bringing her closer into me.

"It's okay, you can tell me."

"It's so stupid. All these years I'd built up this dream in my head. I imagined us finding each other and falling in love. You were going to be searching for me because you just had to find me. You'd take one look at me and fall madly in love. But you only seem to want the kids, you've done all this for them and I feel like a horrible mother because that should be enough but somehow it isn't, because I want you to want me too."

I shouldn't laugh. I knew if I did she'd take it the wrong way. I turned her onto her back and looked down at her. "Is that what's bothering you? Do you really think that I only did all this for our kids? Do you know how many ways I could've done this that wouldn't have had to involve us getting married? I snowed you sweetheart."

She picked her head up and looked at me with her red swollen eyes. "What do you mean?"
"I mean, that I took one look at you in that mall and the memories started flooding in. I may not have remembered everything about you in the past few years, but those memories kept me going for a long time."

"If I'd known anyway to find you, I would've and that's before I knew about the kids. I want you as much as I want them. More than that, I want to have more children with you. Lots and lots of babies." I started moving inside her again.

"Do you need me to say the words? Are you so blind that you can't see?" She pulled my head down to hers and we both got lost in that kiss.

I didn't know I was in love with her until she cried. Didn't have the words to describe what I'd been feeling all this time. I chased those memories in my head for a long time. Each time I woke up from one of those dreams, every time I got a flash of that night, the feelings were there. But how was I to know what they were?

I was so confused back then, so mixed up with grief. I'd just lost my family and ended up in bed with a stranger. A stranger whose scent had stayed with me even when I couldn't remember who she was.

Seeing her last night had been a miracle. Even before I'd seen the twins hiding behind her, it was her that I'd been drawn to, her I'd walked towards as the memories started to unfold.

It's not easy for me to show what's in my heart. Not easy to say those words, but I know what I feel, know that I couldn't imagine life without her in it the way she is now. For me that's more than enough.

I spent the rest of the night showing her just how much until we both fell into a deep sleep wrapped in each other's arms.

***

"They're up." I heard the kids the next morning as they rushed the door. I'd only just opened my eyes and nudged their mother for some early morning nookie when I heard their little feet and voices outside the door.

It was snowing again but the room was still warm from the fire that needed a good stoking. I reached down to the bottom of the bed and nabbed the robes we'd put on during the night when we went down to raid the kitchen and put their million and one gifts under the tree.

We barely had enough time to shove our arms into them before the door was pushed open and we were under attack. They both threw themselves onto the bed and I dodged little arms and legs and they snuck under the covers for a cuddle.

Isabella was looking a little down in the mouth since both babies were climbing all over me after giving her a good morning kiss. "Come on daddy." My daughter tried to pull me out of bed with her brother's help.

"We're coming let daddy get his slippers." I got out of bed and slipped my feet into my slippers before picking them up, one in each hand. "Take your time sweetheart. I'll feed these two then come up and get dressed."

She smiled and waved us off. "Okay you two you'll have breakfast and then you get to open gifts."

"Aww daddy." My little princess turned my face to hers and stared me down. "We not hungry." She passed that glare to her brother to get him to go along.

"Nice try but you have to eat first." She haggled with me all the way to the kitchen and it didn't help that we had to pass the room with the tree and the mountain of gifts that covered half the room.

"Look Luca, Santa came." She kicked her little feet and clapped her hands in glee. I was tempted to let them...oh what the hell.

I took them into the room and let them loose. Their squeals and screams of glee were well worth the wrath I was sure to incur when their mom and mine came downstairs.

I felt like a dad. There's no feeling in the world like it. Shit! "Hey kids wait one second, daddy forgot the camera." What an ass, of course I wanted to record this; our first Christmas together.

I passed mom and dad on my way upstairs. "Morning, be right back." They laughed as I rushed past them. My wife was putting on her shoes as I ran into the room and straight to the closet for the camera I'd put there last night.

"What's going on where're the kids?"

"Hurry or you'll miss all the fun. Your daughter suckered me into letting them forego breakfast so they can go straight to the gifts." She shook her head like I was a lost cause as I left the room.

Back downstairs the kids were pawing through their loot while grandma and grandpa kept them company. They saw me with the camera stuck to my face and started digging in.

"Here son give me that, you go join them." Dad took the camera and I joined my kids on the floor as their mom came in. "Come get in on this honey." I held a hand out to her and helped her sit next to me on the floor.

"Mommy look, look momma." I laughed at their antics as they showed us each and every toy as it was revealed. Luca wanted to ride his new bike, and ma who would've skinned me alive if I even tried, let him ride in the house because there was snow on the ground outside.

My little princess was more interested in her doll that was as tall as she was and who spoke in three languages. "I see no one plans to eat breakfast in this house today." Aggie came into the living room with a tray of coffee for the adults and hot chocolate with a mountain of whip cream on top.

"No fair, where's my chocolate?" Aggie makes the best hot chocolate from real chocolate and milk and enough sugar to keep a horse going. "Coming right up." She left the room and my wife frowned over her coffee. "Don't worry sweetheart, I'll share."

Chapter 15

BELLA

***

It was by far the most amazing Christmas my kids or I have ever had. There was so much laughter and warmth. Not that we didn't have fun at mom's but with Melissa there-there was always tension in the air, and my parents in their quest to keep the peace, always made sure my kids didn't get anything more than my nephew or my sister would have a fit.

Here all the focus was on them, and they shone. There was no one taking their stuff, no aunt to inspect their loot before they could actually get to play with them. And the best part of all, even with all the new shiny gifts, their dad was their main attraction.

I watched them run to him to show him some new trick with one of their new toys. He was so funny, he always involved me in whatever it was as if he thought I was feeling left out.

I will admit that this morning in bed when they'd been all over him it had been a bit of a shock. But when I'd had a nice shower and the rock on my finger blinded me in the mirror my mind cleared and I was able to put things in perspective.

Last night, I had stopped him from saying the words after I'd stupidly spilled my guts. I didn't want him to say them just because I had. I wasn't sure what it was that he felt for me, but he had a point. There were a million other ways he could've handled the situation. The fact that he'd married me must mean something.

I loved the way he was with our kids. Loved that my little girl had her daddy and that my boy had someone to look up to. They were so in love with him it was silly.

"Look daddy, it sings." My little princess showed her dad her new doll as she plopped her little butt down on his lap. "Let's hear it princess." They spent five minutes on that before she was off to something else and then it was Luca's turn, and so it went all morning until they tired themselves out.

"That was spectacular." He picked me up and swung me around in the room as his parents looked on. "I love you Mrs. Deleon." Now that was unprovoked and heartfelt, at least I felt it in my heart. And the way he stopped as he said it and just looked at me like he was seeing me for the first time, I knew he meant it.

I hugged him hard enough to break him. "I love you too."

"What do you say we go take a nap while the kids are down? I'm a little tired myself." He whispered the words in my ear making me blush and hide my face in his neck as he started out of the room.

"We'll see you two later. I suggest you get your second wind before the thunderstorms wake up from their nap." He took me upstairs to his room where I thought we were going to make love, but instead he put me down and got a few pillows and a blanket and placed them before the fire.

He lit a fire before turning on the stereo in his room and putting on Christmas music. I took his hand when he reached for me and laid in front of him.

"Tell me more about them." We got settled and I told him every little detail about their lives. All the little quirks and mannerisms. "They seem so well rounded already, thank you for that."

"Oh, they came like that. I didn't have to do much. I don't know. Maybe it's because they're twins, but they're so happy with one another that it's kept them out of trouble. They can go for hours just playing quietly together and then some days I think the gates of hell have opened up and released the hound."

"Luca's pretty laid back, kind of like you. But your daughter, now she can be a handful."

"Not my little princess, she's the most darling little girl I've ever met. And so smart."

"Yeah? Wait 'til you tell her no." I laughed at his look of superiority. He just knew that he knew it all. "I guess I'll just never tell her no."

"Oh ho, that ought to go over swell in her teen years."
"I didn't give you your gift yet, I was waiting until we were alone." I held up my finger. "I thought this was it." He got up and went to the nightstand drawer.

"I had my lawyer fax this over last night." He handed me a sheaf of papers before rejoining me. I read the paper twice before it registered what I was looking at.

"What does this mean? It says you've made me half owner of everything you own, that can't be right." Was he insane? Who is this guy?

"It's right alright. Took me half an hour while you were asleep to convince him to do it. Like you he thought I was making a mistake but I know exactly what I'm doing."

"But…why?"
"Because you need to know that I won't use my money to take our kids. You need to believe that I'm with you because I want to be."

"I can't accept this Luca. I already told you that I love you I don't need this to prove anything."

"Good, you can keep it in a safe place for those days when you lose your mind."

"And now that-that's out of the way." He rolled me onto my back and slid between my thighs. "Hello Mrs. Deleon. I didn't get my good morning kiss." He was taking me clothes off as he spoke and I returned the favor.

He used his mouth and fingers to bring me to fever pitch before sliding inside me. "You think they'll let me finish before busting down the door?"
"Welcome to fatherhood…daddy."

***

We fell asleep in front of the fire with him still inside me as we laid on our sides. I woke up to him stroking into me from behind and squeezed the hand holding my breast.

"You're awake." He kissed my cheek as he stroked into me and my only answer was to push back into him. "Did I tell you how much I love fucking you?" His words worked like an aphrodisiac on my senses and before I knew it I was doing something I'd never done before.

"Hey, where're you going?" I pulled off of him and now I was the one in control. I was the one pushing him to his back. I took his cock in my hand, wet with my juices and pre-cum.

Looking into his eyes like a sultry siren I licked his tip. I saw the change come over him just before I covered his cockhead with my mouth and sucked until my cheeks concaved.

For an encore I slid my mouth all the way down his cock until it hit the back of my throat. "Oh shit, oh fuck." He grabbed my hair and started pumping up into my mouth until he jumped in my mouth. "I'm going to cum baby pull off."

I clamped down harder and just went with it. My hand cupped his balls as I worked my throat around his cock and soon I tasted his salty cum in my mouth.

He growled louder than I've ever heard and grabbed my head hard enough to hurt but I didn't care. I let him slip out of my mouth when he was done, and moved to lie beside him but he had other ideas.

He pulled me up his body and lifted me over his face until his mouth was clamped over me and just like that, as soon as I felt his tongue inside me, I came.

He kept it up until I came twice more and I begged for mercy. "Please, no more."
'That's fine I'll do all the work." "What was he talking about, no way he could go again.

I soon found I was wrong when he pushed me to my hands and knees and slammed into me. This was fast becoming my favorite position. I could feel more of him this way.

"When we get home where you can rest up for a few days, I'm going to ass fuck you." Oh shit. I'd never thought of that before, but those words said in his voice made me cum so hard he wasn't in time to catch my scream this time.

We barely got cleaned up and out of the room just as the kids were waking up from their nap. We had another round of playtime before it was time for my parents to come over.

I was hoping against hope that Melissa wouldn't come, but I should've known she wouldn't pass up the opportunity.

"Baby, what's wrong? Why are you so tense all of a sudden?" How can he know me so well already? I thought I was hiding it very well.

"It's nothing, I'm just hoping all goes well tonight." "Why wouldn't it?" I shrugged and changed the subject and it was soon forgotten. I even got caught up in the stories his parents told about his wayward ways as a child, which he swore were all fabrications.

When the bell rang, I almost jumped out of my skin but Luca was watching my every move so I controlled it. I heard my mom's voice when Aggie opened the door while the rest of us waited.

I had a bad feeling in the pit of my gut when they all walked into the living room where we were sitting until dinner. Melissa was already looking around with that look on her face.

Luca took my hand and squeezed gently as if he understood, but how could he? I'd never told him anything about her treatment of me, and his kids.

Introductions were made and I was glad that she at least had enough class not to ask them how much money they had, though it was close.

By the time we sat down to dinner I was a nervous wreck. I'd watched my nephew paw through my kids' stuff laying claim to anything he wished, but Luca was on top of it. He sternly but gently told Axel that the toys belonged to Luca and Luna and maybe next time we'll get him some of his own toys.

"You didn't get your nephew anything?" Melissa turned a glare my way.

"His stuff is at mom's I haven't had time to wrap them because we've been here."

"What that cheap crap you buy every year?" I could've sunk through the floor I was that embarrassed. Even the beautiful and cheery music couldn't remove the ugly she'd brought with her.

Thankfully it was then that Aggie announced dinner and nothing else was said, but I could see from the tic in his jaw that Luca was not pleased.

We sat down to dinner and gratefully nothing else was said about it. The kids were well behaved but a little reserved now that she was here and I felt bad that their jaw was tainted.

"Okay kids, it's time to clean up and then it's pajama time." We'd had dinner early but I was using their bedtime as an excuse to get my family out of there before Melissa drank anymore than she had at dinner. I didn't trust all those trips to the bathroom she'd taken and my nerves were shot.

"Come on sis, I'll help you." Uh oh, that can't be good; she's never offered to help with anything to do with the kids before. I couldn't very well deny her in front of everyone so I said nothing as she followed me out of the room.

We were barely up the stairs and out of earshot of the others when her true purpose was revealed. My three year old going on thirty year old kids decided they wanted to undress themselves so I left them to it in the nursery while I headed into the bathroom to run their bath.

"So, what are you gonna do for me?"

"What?"

"I'm your sister, remember, and you just fell in the gravy. How do you think these rich people would feel if they knew you had a sister in need and refused to help her? They don't strike me as the type to look too kindly on that kind of behavior sister dear.

"You're crazy, first of all, their money is not mine and I'm not about to take anything from them to give to you." I can't believe she was bringing this here. Especially today of all days.

"Oh get off it. You may have fooled the rest of them but you don't fool me. You found the first rich dupe you could sink your talons in and pawned your spawn off on him. As if he'd have looked at you twice if you hadn't lied and told him he was their father." Did he sign a pre-nup?"

"That's not…" I started to defend myself but was cut off by Luca. "I will thank you not to speak to my wife like that in her home. Are you high-I'm guessing you are-I noticed it as soon as you walked in. To answer your question, this dupe knows his own and if I'd had any doubts, there's always DNA testing."

"I was talking to my sister."

No, you were speaking to my wife and I think you called my children spawns. Needless to say, I don't like you. My wife has been a nervous wreck all day because of your impending visit, now I see why. You'll make your excuses to the others and leave my home. You're not welcome."

"Luca…" He held his hand up and I zipped it. "Go take care of the children, I'll see to this." I wasn't sure I should leave them alone together but the look on his face didn't leave room for argument.

By the time I came back with the kids, they were gone and I was miserable. My parents came up to say goodbye and apologized for her behavior but nothing was said and I left it until I could speak to mom in private.

Luca came back to held get the kids ready for bed, and by the time he was through reading one of their new story books I was laughing along with the kids at the voices he made.

"Good night mommy, goodnight daddy." After hugs and kisses, we turned down the light and went back downstairs. His parents were gone so we sat in front of the fire with a glass of wine.

"Did you have a good day?"
"Yes. Except for that little issue with my sister. What did you say to her after I left?"
"Nothing much; tell me, have you always let her bully you?" I grew a bit tense by that and tried pulling away but his arm came around my shoulder holding me in place.

"I've never understood people's willingness to excuse bad behavior just because someone came with a title. It took me less than five minutes to see what she was. And I'm sure this wasn't the first time she's spoken that way about my kids. Add the fact that her own son is a terror who obviously has experience manhandling my children and I have to tell you I'm not a fan."

"She wasn't…" I was about to lie but caught myself. It's true we've always made excuses for her and maybe he was right, maybe it was time we stopped. "I know you're right. It was just always easier to let things slide."

"Well, now you have me and no one is ever going to speak to you that way again. I won't stand for it." He had that tic going in his jaw again. "Hey let's not let her spoil our day."

"She can't, I'm just hoping you know that." He hugged me close and kissed my forehead and we both turned to gaze at the fire. It was peaceful and gave me time to think. I haven't done much of that lately. Everything seemed to be moving at warp speed.

We were both silent, lost in our own thoughts and I took the time to go over the last three days in my head. I have to admit to being happier than I've ever been and that sickening fear that had plagued me in the beginning was gone now.

He'd gone above and beyond in a few short days not just for the kids, but for me as well. Suddenly, I couldn't wait for the holidays to be over so we could go to New York.

"What's New York like?" He smiled and settled back on the couch, drawing me closer in his arms. "You're going to love it..." he went on to tell me all about the things he'd found to love in the big city, and by the time he was through, I was half in love with the place myself.

We sat down there most of the night whispering to one another, making plans for the future. As the fire burned down in the grate and the lights from the tree casted shadows on the wall, I felt safe and secure in the safety of his arms. I'd got my own special Christmas miracle.

Epilogue

LUCA

***

"Luna Juliana Deleon, get your little butt in here." I will not laugh-I will not laugh. I repeated the mantra to myself as I heard her running towards me. She'd grown about an inch in the last year. Four years old and full of spit and vinegar.

"Yes daddy." She looked towards the crib where her little sister slept and back at me. She wasn't adjusting very well to the new addition. The day we brought little Belle home she told us to take her back. There were screaming fits and tears and for a while there she wouldn't let me out of her sight.

She didn't mind sharing me with her brother who was in love with his new little sister, but if I held the baby she'd have a fit. I don't know how she does it, but I could be in another room and without fail she'd know that I was holding Belle and she'd come after me.

I've done everything I can to get her to understand but nothing any of the books say work. But this one was a bit much. I saw the for sale sign as soon as I came into the room. I guess that's what we get for encouraging them to learn. They're both frighteningly intelligent for their age, which was good since it got them into the best Pre-School in the city without having to do a stint on the waiting list.

But it led to things like this. "Did you do this?" I pulled the taped sign off the crib where she'd stuck it. Her little face was set and she rolled her eyes towards the crib. "Yes. I don't see why we have to keep her. Lana's cat had kittens and they gave them all away."

"Oh, so now your sister is a kitten?" I've heard it all now. Her mom seems to think it will pass but after three months with no let up I wasn't too sure. I picked her up and that smile on her face told the story. She didn't like her daddy to show affection to anyone else.

"Guess what I did today at school daddy, wanna see?" I knew her game; she wanted me out of that room and away from Belle. Instead, I went to the rocking chair in the corner and sat with her on my lap.

"Princess, why don't you like your sister?" I've tried reasoning with her before but maybe this time I'll get through to her. She shrugged her little shoulders and laid her head on my chest.

"I don't know daddy."
"Do you want mommy and daddy to be sad?" She picked her head up and looked at me with her beautiful eyes. "No daddy."
"But if you sell Belle then mommy and daddy will be really sad."
"You cry daddy?"

"Yes baby daddy would cry. You don't want daddy to cry do you?"

She looked towards the crib and then huffed out a heavy sigh as though she had the weight of the world on her shoulders. "So, can we keep her?"

"I guess."

"And will you help mommy and daddy take care of her? Will you be a big sister and teach her all the things mommy and daddy taught you?"

She gave it some thought but didn't give me an answer then and there. I guess when the time comes I can pass my business off to her without a thought. She's going to make one shrewd business woman.

"Can I have ice cream now?" I wasn't falling for that shit again. "What did mommy say?" She got real quiet and changed the subject. "Guess what Luca did daddy." Uh huh. Dealing with her was like walking through a minefield.

"Let's go see what your brother and mother are up to." I carried her downstairs where her mom was in the kitchen helping her brother with a school project. As much time as those two spend together you'd think my boy was a mama's boy, but to this day they both still cling to me. I was worried after a while that they had some kind of abandonment issue. Like they were afraid that I would disappear from their lives again, but their mother convinced me that I was being paranoid.

"Hi son." I kissed my boy's hair and accepted his kiss to the cheek. "Hi dad, look at what me and mom did, isn't it great?" It was the same lava flowing project every kid had been doing on science class since before my time. The only difference is I was a little older than him when I did mine.

This school they were in worries me sometimes with the shit they have these kids doing. If they weren't so smart I'd probably be looking for alternatives, but everyone agreed their little minds needed to be constantly stimulated or they'd get into more shit than they do now.

"This is perfect son, good job. How was school today?" I kissed my wife in passing which was all I seemed to get these days until the little stinkers went to bed. And usually as soon as they were down their sister woke up needing to be fed.

Not that I'm complaining about that, I get a lot of enjoyment from the leftovers. But it feels like forever since I had her all to myself. The holidays were coming up again soon and we were getting ready to head to New Hampshire in a few days.

New York was already decked out, seems like they start earlier every year, but I didn't care. This year was gearing up to be even better than the last, because now I get to share everything with the people I love most in this world from beginning to end.

The kids have already dragged me to FAO Swartz a thousand times since it wasn't that far from our apartment. They like to look at the window display at night when all the hustle of bustle was over and the city was taking its rest.

We went through the nightly ritual of nobody wanting to go to bed after bath time and the bedtime stories that followed after, and then it was mommy and daddy time once we'd looked in on the new little princess.

"Your daughter is trying to sell her sister again." I rubbed the towel over my hair as I came into the bedroom.

"Oh really, I thought we were past that."

"I told you."

"Oh dear, something must have set her off, she was getting better."

"What could've set her off? Did you do something different?"

"No. Oh I bet I know what it is. Your mom sent something in the mail today."

"So? She usually sends each of them something in the mail when she does that."

"Well, you know how your mom wanted Belle to be christened in your gown? It came today. I was on the phone with your mom and mine going on and on about it, and Luna was in and out of the room. That must've been it."

"Well I had another talk with her but we'll see." I dropped the towel and walked over to where she was sitting brushing her hair in the mirror.

"And how was your day?" I massaged her shoulders and she moaned with pleasure. "Oh that feels so good." "We should schedule a session sometime this weekend." A nice his and her massage usually led to very nice things.

My obsession with her body hadn't abated not even a little bit and now after the baby, she's even more ripe. Her breasts, which were always a source of great pleasure, were my latest vice. I think I have my lips wrapped around her nipple more than the baby. I can't help it.

If you put her milk in a cup, I wouldn't touch that shit with a ten-foot pole. But straight from the source, that shit keeps my dick hard as flint.

I worked my hands down her chest until I cupped her and just the feel of her pebbled nipples under my palm was enough. I pulled her up from the chair and turned her around in my arms.

The last year has been nothing short of miraculous. After all her fears of settling in, it had taken her less than a month to fall in love with the place. I'd given her carte blanche to turn my once bachelor pad into a home fit for a family and she did with the help of designers and contractors who came in and reshaped things the way she wanted.

Now our home was decorated in the holiday spirit and she was the one bemoaning the fact that we had to leave the city to go back home for the holidays.

New York really was something to see this time of year. Something I'd missed my first few years here but I didn't feel too badly about that, because seeing it through their eyes, hers and our children's was better than anything I could've enjoyed alone.

I held her precious face in my hands as we stood next to the bed and kissed her with all the love I held in my heart for her. She'd turned the stereo system on when we came in and the strains of Christmas melodies were already floating through the air.

With the fire going, the music playing, and the twinkling lights coming through the windows, it was like being transported back in time.

This year, instead of dreams that left me wanting and empty, I wake up to her warm body in my arms and our children just a few doors down. "I love you." I never get tired of saying it, or hearing the sweet words from her lips. She'd outgrown her fear of me not wanting her, not really loving her, because I've used every opportunity to show her.

Last year this time, I would never have believed that I'd ever have this or anything like it. But in just a few short days, we'll be celebrating our one-year anniversary, and that year had only given me hope for more to come.

"I wonder how are you going to top last year's gift?" I grinned down at her as I took her down to the bed and slid into her waiting heat. "I bet you can't." She wrapped her arms around me and gave me one of her special secretive smiles. The one I usually get just before she zings me.

"I'm pregnant." My already hard cock grew in fullness as I pulled back to look down at her. "You…" She nodded as I lost my voice. Words cannot express how I felt at that moment. I'd enjoyed every minute of her pregnancy. Because I'd missed her time with the twins, I'd gone all in and found that I loved her more then than ever.

Her pregnancy had brought out something in me that I didn't even know I had. I was already so overprotective of her and the kids, but when she came back from the doctor's and gave me the news, I'd gone into overdrive.

There's no feeling like knowing your woman is ripening with your seed. Watching it grow inside her, feeling it kick against your hand. I get harder just thinking about it.

"You're sure, you went to the doctor?" I moved inside her because I couldn't not, and before she could answer, I was kissing her. Of course she was sure, she was an old hand at this.

She moved beneath me, opening herself up more, letting me go deeper inside her. Her kiss was more ravenous, almost desperate with need. She too gets very affected by her pregnancy. She once told me it was like carrying around a part of me inside her all day, and the feelings were indescribable.

I moved my hand between us and covered my little boy or girl as I stroked into her over and over with our mouths fused. "I don't want to hurt you." I'm always afraid when she's carrying one of my children that I'll hurt her when we make love. I remember how tight, how small she was before I opened her up enough to take my whole length, and the problem is that I lose control when I knew my child is inside her no matter how I tell myself not to.

"We're fine you won't hurt us. I promise, now love me the way you know you want to, the way I want you to." When she grinned up at me and bit into her lip seductively I should've known she was up to something. She pushed me back and I slipped out of her and then she was on her knees looking over her shoulder at me.

"Oh yeah." I pressed down on her ass and opened her pinkness a little wider for my mouth and tongue. Her taste was still unbeatable and I lapped up her juices as they flowed from her body while my cock dripped pre-cum onto the mattress.

Pulling my tongue out of her, I licked up to her clit and back to her slit and over again until I couldn't bear to be outside of her a minute longer. I gritted my teeth against the need to slam home and went nice and slow.

Then she gave me just what I needed. Looking over her shoulder she looked me in the eye and said, "fuck me Luca." Then she bit her lip and I was lost. All control left me and I just went with emotion and feeling. With her hips held firmly in my hands, I let go and gave her what she repeatedly begged me for.

I kept one hand over her tummy as I hit her from behind with the other over her mouth because she was still a screamer. "I'm close baby." She ought to know what her words would do to me. I felt the first jet of cum leave me and hit her walls just as she tightened around me. Drawing the rest of my offering from me.

"Merry Christmas, Luca."

Printed in Poland
by Amazon Fulfillment
Poland Sp. z o.o., Wrocław